03

The TEXAS RODEO *Murder*

GEORGE WILHITE

SUNBELT EAKIN  Austin, Texas

FIRST EDITION
Copyright © 2003
By George Wilhite
Published in the United States of America
By Eakin Press
A Division of Sunbelt Media, Inc.
P.O. Drawer 90159
Austin, Texas 78709-0159
email: sales@eakinpress.com
website: www.eakinpress.com
ALL RIGHTS RESERVED.
1   2   3   4   5   6   7   8   9
1-57168-779-3

Library of Congress Control Number: 2003100007

This book is dedicated to three men whose presence in my life made an immeasurable difference.

First was my father, George Sr., who wrote some poems in his youth but never followed that dream. Thanks, Dad. I could never have done it without you; I just wish my first copy was going to you.

Second was Chuck Smith, publisher of Rodeo News *magazine, who was from the old school, much like Jake. He taught me that there's a fine line between living and working and when you can do both at once, you're the luckiest man alive.*

And last, but not least, there was Bob Blackwood, who died way too early. Among many other things, Bob taught me how to teach. His best advice to me was, "God may intend for you to win the world, but you've got to get up off the couch and enter the rodeo."

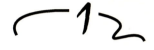

I picked up the phone on the second ring.

"English Department. Ira Carter here."

"It's Jake. Just listen."

Then I heard that annoying tunnel sound of being switched to a speaker phone. I hated those damn things, and Jake knew it. I'd been the editor of his rodeo magazine for five years before I'd gone into teaching at the college, and he'd heard me bitch about them plenty of times. So why did he . . .

"Well, Mr. Lawson," a tinny, disembodied voice said from the earpiece, "it looks like you've been holding out on us."

"I don't know what you're talking about."

"Come on, Lawson, the address. Where is J.D.'s address?"

"I don't have any address. You two better just leave."

A third voice joined in. "Look, Lawson, just give it to us and . . . Damn, he's got the speaker phone on."

There was a loud burst of static and the line went dead.

I dialed the Hillsboro police and told them an assault was taking place at the *Texas Rodeo* magazine office on Hackberry Street and to send someone immediately. The dispatcher was Suzy Hargas, a former student of mine. She started asking the usual bank of questions for such a call.

"Damn it, Suzy, this is Mr. Carter. Get someone over there right now before it's too late."

I slammed the phone down and was out the door before she could reply.

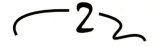

I t was a good fifteen-minute trip from the rural campus of Hill County College to the magazine office behind Jake's house on the opposite side of town. I made it in five. I even beat the police.

I slid to a stop on the gravel drive between the house and the office. No vehicles were there except for Jake's battered old '65 Dodge pickup and the brand new Lincoln he used for high-dollar business trips and entertainment. I reached behind the seat of my truck, pulled out the old Colt revolver I kept there, and made sure it was loaded. Just in case.

The front door was open behind the closed screen door, but I figured that was where someone would expect me to come in, so I headed for the back door of the press room. The magazine had seen better times. The building had a false front, like the stores and saloons you see in reruns of *Gunsmoke* or in Clint Eastwood movies. A wide board porch ran along the front and a sign reading "*Texas Rodeo*," in western-style type, hung above the porch. Originally, it had been painted barn red and the name was in bright yellow. I'd helped Jake paint it twice in the five years I had been there. Image had meant a lot to him and to some of the big, back-East advertisers that bought space in the mag. But the red and yellow was faded, I noticed, and one of the boards on the end of the porch was missing.

Nowadays, Jake was usually alone at the office. He had three or four "field editors" who traveled around the country and wrote stories and took pictures, but they stayed on the road mostly, coming in only once a month to help with the paste-up and relax for a couple of days. Two of my journalism students helped him out part-time, but they worked from 10:00 to 2:00. I checked my watch—3:30. Jake was probably alone in there.

No one was in the press room. The old Heidelberg stood gloomily in the corner, having yielded to a new computerized four-color press Jake had bought last year. The press man wasn't around. He wouldn't be due for another week.

A scratching noise came from Jake's office across the room. Before I checked it, I flung open the door that opened into the receptionist's office/file room/paste-up room. Nobody there. The door to my old office just off the front area was open, and I could see no one was in there either. That left just the bathroom, camera room, and Jake's office. I banked on the fact that nobody would be in either of the first two and headed cautiously for Jake's office. Only thirty seconds or so had passed since I'd arrived.

Jake's office door was open. I slunk down to the ground, thinking I might have a better chance of not being shot if someone was still here. I peeked around the doorframe and almost poked my nose into Jake's eye. He was on the ground and pulling himself to the door.

"They're . . . gone," he gasped, reaching an arm toward me. "Find . . . him."

His head collapsed to the floor. One hand, extended

toward me, held the corner of an envelope with a return address hand-lettered on it. I took it and reached for Jake as I heard the police car siren. I dropped my revolver and tried to turn Jake over, but I couldn't. He was a bull of a man, over six feet tall and close to 275, with only a little of that weight coming from the paunch he carried.

Jake, in his seventies, had won the world title in bull riding back in the '50s and had always been a scrapper, the kind of cowboy that movie stereotypes were made of. But he'd been smart enough to start the magazine before he'd quit riding, and it had kept him living in pretty high cotton until just the last few years, when animal rights groups started trying to knock rodeo. Most of their claims were based on their own ignorance of the sport and its equipment, and the ones that weren't dealt with issues that the sport tried to prevent with heavy fines. Jake had used the magazine to fight off such groups twice before, in the '70s and early '80s, but the last few years he lacked the strength to take them on again. He'd been trying to talk me into coming back to the magazine, even part-time, to help him with them, but I'd declined twice. I couldn't help but think that if I had come back, I might have been there to help this time.

I got him turned over, and that's when I saw the blood from the gunshot wound. It was a raw, bloody, ragged wound, too big and messy to be caused by a handgun. The ragged edges were probably from a shotgun, the pellets having spread out as they hit, making the jagged perimeter of the wound. With a gutshot, he'd probably die.

The cop came storming around the corner with his gun out, looking for people at eye level. He almost stumbled over us. I could have shot him three or four times before he ever saw me.

"You . . . You . . . just hold it right there," he stammered.

At least he didn't yell, "Reach for the sky, hombre," I thought.

The confusion lasted only a few minutes until the chief of police arrived. Bill Lee and I had rodeoed together a few years back, and he was a pretty good bareback rider. He calmly explained to his officer that Jake had been shot with a shotgun and I was carrying a .45. He also noticed that my gun hadn't been fired. Then he listened to my explanation as the EMTs got Jake onto the stretcher.

The old fart was still alive but unconscious. They didn't even bother with the clinic in Hillsboro, but headed straight for the Waco hospital, thirty miles south. Bill nodded to my silent request to go along.

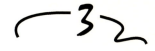

In the ambulance ride all the way to Waco, Jake never spoke. I wouldn't have been allowed to get in the meat wagon in a big city, but here in Hillsboro everyone knew everyone else, and Bucky Blake never even said a word when I stepped into the back of the ambulance.

Bucky had been the one who hauled me in the night I'd taken the horn in the face. I'd been clowning the Hillsboro rodeo, and the first bull out on the first night had been a hangup. A big, brindle "swamp bull," he'd thrown the bull rider down over his head, turned him around with a horn, and got the rider's hand twisted over so he couldn't let go if he'd wanted to. Of course, at that point in time, the horn had knocked him cold. I'd gone in and gotten the tail of his bull rope and was jerked off my feet when it didn't come loose. With my feet back under me, I stuck my cleats in the ground and leaned back with all my weight on the rope. The wrap came loose, the cow-boy came loose, and I ended up on one knee. The brindle had been cagey, and he got in a lucky punch that caught me in the jaw, breaking it in seven places, the doctor told me later while he was wiring me up.

Bucky looked up at me from his spot beside Jake.

"Ira? He's pretty bad, you know."

I nodded, but didn't say anything.

"He may not make it."

"I know, Bucky. It's okay. I know y'all will do whatever you can."

Bucky gave me a tight-lipped sympathy smile and turned back to his work.

I liked that about him. We'd seen each other a lot until I quit fighting bulls and started doing barrel work and comedy acts. He'd learned early on that all I asked for was the truth. I didn't want sugar coating. Just tell me what the hell the situation is, then it's up to me to handle it.

We pulled up to the Hillcrest Medical Center emergency room, where two or three doctors or interns waited on the curb. We had barely stopped when the back door opened from the outside and Dr. Harry Lipscomb stuck his shaggy head inside the ambulance.

"Pretty bad, huh, Ira?" he said, merely glancing at me as he helped Bucky get Jake out.

"Yeah, Griz, shotgun. Close range. In the gut."

Jake and I had started calling the doctor Grizzly Adams because of his wild head of hair and full beard. He looked more like a mountain man than a trauma surgeon, but he was one of the best. He had to be or they never would have allowed him to keep the hair. Since Griz had come to the hospital's ER, its fatalities from auto wrecks, knife fights, and shootings had dropped drastically. He'd been a medic in Vietnam, pretty much fresh out of high school.

"I'll do what I can for him, Ira. No promises, though."

"That's okay, Griz. You'll do your best."

He broke off the conversation and started dictating orders to the two interns who now had the gurney. They disappeared into the brightly lit triage area of the ER.

Dr. Lipscomb had wired my jaw shut the night Bucky had hauled me in. When he'd handed me the tiny wire snippers, I knew he'd worked on cowboys before.

"Now, I know you aren't going to listen to what I tell you to do," he'd said, "so keep these in a pocket so you can cut the wires if you start to throw up when you get drunk or in case they need to keep you from swallowing your tongue if you get knocked out tomorrow night." I'd kept the wire cutters in my pocket until he took the wires off, and then I'd handed them back "for the next hard-headed cowboy who needs 'em," I told him.

I made my way to the admissions desk, where a flustered nurse was waiting impatiently for me, tapping one foot while holding about a foot-thick sheaf of papers.

"I suppose you're Mr. Carter?" she demanded.

"Yes, ma'am."

"Dr. Lipscomb said you'd be able to give me the information we need. We can't just take someone into the emergency room without having the proper forms signed and—"

"All that stuff's in your computer, ma'am. His name is Jake Lawson. Look him up. You print it out and I'll sign it. Just like I did the last time we were here. And the time before that. And the one before that. When you're done, I'll be in the cafeteria."

I turned my back on her and started off.

"But—" she started from behind me.

I whirled around a little too quick and a little too angry. "*But* . . . that man is dying, lady. I couldn't care less about your damned forms and procedures. You've got all the information nine ways to Sunday sitting in that computer of yours. Now, leave me alone before I bite your prudish little head right off."

I stormed off and headed to the cafeteria for a cup of

coffee. I needed something stronger, but caffeine would have to do for the moment.

I carried the biggest cup of coffee they had to the ER waiting room. Three of those cups later, the prissy nurse brought me a much-less imposing stack of papers to sign, with all the places I needed to sign highlighted in yellow. I signed them and dropped them off to her on my way back for yet another cup of coffee. I was adding to my growing collection of styrofoam cups beside my chair when Griz came out of the operating room. He had already taken his mask and gloves off, and he was shaking his head as he approached.

"We've done all we can, Ira. But you know how bad it was. Shotgun pellets tore up a lot of intestine. All that toxic matter in the intestines is spread to hell and gone inside there. There's just so much damage that we can't get it fixed. He's got a few minutes, maybe an hour. I thought you'd want to know and be there with him." He put a hand on my shoulder.

I nodded and mumbled a heartfelt but nearly silent "Thanks, Griz" before following him back in. He pointed to the room where they were taking Jake, and I went in without a word. Griz headed on to other emergencies.

They brought Jake in and made him as comfortable as possible. The morphine drip served as evidence that he was near the end. I glanced at the clock. It was 10:15.

After they left, I moved the chair close to the hospital bed and wondered if I should hold his hand or not. It wasn't something the crusty old bastard would do or tolerate if he was conscious, but then I'd always heard that dying people wanted the touch of a fellow human being. I thought about it a while and decided Jake was Jake, and he didn't hold by the same rules that all other humans did. In the end, I just sat and talked to him so he'd know I was there, just in case he could hear me. I talked about how glad I was to have come to work for him and how much of an impression he'd made on me. Stuff that most guys wouldn't dare say to another guy under any other circumstances.

Just before midnight, Jake took one of those deep, shuddering breaths that precede death. I looked at him. His eyes flickered for a moment, rested on me for a second, then his lips parted. His hand reached for mine and held it tightly in his clenched fist. With his death grip on my hand, he said only one thing before he died.

"Ira," he whispered hoarsely, barely audible, "find . . . him."

42

Jake's words haunted me the next morning. I barely made it through the first two classes of the day. At 10:00 I went to my office and closed the door. I thought about locking it, but decided against it. After all, this was the last day of classes and students were handing in their final projects. I just closed the door and sat down in front of a blank computer screen.

I hadn't flipped on the overhead light, on purpose, but I did reach over to turn on a floor lamp. The torchiere lamp that threw light at the ceiling had three settings, and I usually kept it on the lowest one. The effect was a "gloomy dungeon," according to one of my fellow instructors, but I liked it that way, especially when I was thinking.

Kicking my feet up on my desk corner, I could see the National Finals Rodeo number, dated 1957, framed above the computer terminal. It had hung in my office at *Rodeo* magazine. Jake had told me he had two of them once, one from '57 and one from '56. Couldn't remember what happened to the other one. I'd always liked that. It wasn't one of the modern, screen-printed, fancy numbers contestants get at the Finals nowadays. It was plain, heavy paper, printed in basic red and black ink. In many ways, Jake's world of rodeo had been simpler, easier. And yet, the men from that time had been tougher, harder. Not only had they needed to be tough in the arena, but they often had to be tough outside of it. He'd told me about the fights with city toughs back East, and how the cowboys had to prove how strong they were at nearly every town they visited. Seems there was always some smartass who thought riding broncs and bulls didn't make a man tough. Jake had agreed.

"It wasn't the riding that made us tough," he used to say. "We had to be tough already just to survive back then."

He and his pard had learned to live on almost nothing. Winnings went for fees at the next rodeo, and that was about all.

"I remember winning one show and getting $42," he'd said. "Paid our gas to the next one and paid the fees. That was it. And there was a whole lot of times I didn't win nothing, not even $42."

There were tradeoffs, though. He'd admitted it. Cowboys nowadays were riding bulls that were tougher to ride than the ones back then.

"They done got scientific on us," he'd once said. "Leverage, torque, centrifugal force, all that. But you still got to be there. It don't matter whether you rode 'em back then or you ride 'em now; you're still not like everyone else, no matter what."

I looked to one side of the number at some of my own artifacts—a photo of me on a bareback horse, another on a bull, the rare one of me on a saddle bronc in college, and still another of me fighting bulls in Arizona. There was the buckle from Madison Square Garden the year the International Professional Rodeo Association held the first rodeo there in five years, and beside it was the group picture they always took at the Garden. I searched the photo with squinted eyes and picked myself out of the background. Back row, third from the right, my arm around Monk Adams from Fort Worth and Campbell "Campy" Lewis of San Antonio. I smiled at my handlebar mustache and the hair over my ears. But they were nothing compared to Monk's Wild Bill goatee and almost shoulder-length hair. Campy, as always, had traditional cowboy-style hair—short, shaved at the ears and neck, and no facial hair to speak of.

Three faces over was the man I was looking for. John Davis—J.D. to every cowboy from Texas to Canada—stood smiling and hipshot at the end of the line. J.D. had been so clean-shaven his jaw practically glowed, and I could see only a thin line of the dark black hair between hat and ears. He was a tall man, unusual for a rough stock rider, despite the image most folks carry of a cowboy. Tall men have to fight forces of leverage and centrifugal force more than short men do. A bull or bronc gets less whip-down or whatever you want to call it on a man who's 5'7 than on a 6'2 rider. I know. I stand at exactly 6'2. So did J.D. We'd talked about it one night after the Finals in Tulsa. We'd been comparing notes.

"Big man has to work twice as hard to make the same ride a smaller man makes," he'd said. "But it's worth it. And there's always been good hands that were tall."

We'd talked about Pete Knight, who, back in the early days of rodeo, was one of the best bronc riders ever. He was tall and rode with enormously long stirrups, against the norm. And J.D. had echoed Jake's words: "Cowboys ain't the norm."

I think he was right.

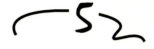

I met Bill just after my last class, around noon, at the café just down the street from the police station. All he could tell me was that it looked like an apparent robbery. The office safe had been opened, and most of the papers in Jake's office had been scattered.

"Looks like they were looking for something. He say anything might clue us in on what they were looking for?"

I shook my head. "No. They just said something about him holding out on them and they wanted to know where it was."

My explanation the day before had been that Jake had called, put me on the speaker phone, and then had been disconnected when one of the men noticed the phone on. I hadn't said anything about their request for an address or about Jake's having handed me one.

"He was able to say there were two of them. That's all."

I trusted Bill, but Jake had called me. He'd handed the address to me. He hadn't called the police or said anything about calling them. I didn't know what was up, but

I thought it might be personal. If it was embarrassing, I owed him that much.

Bill offered his condolences, saying the body should be released later that day and that I might want to make the arrangements since there was no family left.

As he walked out, my mind started churning again. I'd been thinking about it all night since I couldn't sleep anyway. The two men had wanted J.D.'s address. That could be anybody. But the one name that kept coming back to me was the John Davis in my picture, the one who had won both the saddle bronc and all-around world championships three years before. A month after he'd won the titles, his bloody pickup had been found half in and half out of a lake near his home in western Oklahoma. The blood had definitely been J.D.'s, and the medical examiner said that there was so much of it that he couldn't possibly have survived. Even if the wound had not been fatal, J.D. had lost almost all of the blood in his body. His wife and two young sons had moved back to live with her family on the reservation in New Mexico.

John had met her at the Santa Fe rodeo. He was one-quarter Comanche and so was she. She was also half Hopi. She and John had lived in Oklahoma, out in the middle of nowhere. Every year he traveled into Colorado and New Mexico during hunting season to do guide work. That and his rodeo winnings had made up the bulk of his income. He and Linda had also done a lot of custom beading and leatherwork to supplement that income. Three years back, he'd decided he could win the world, so he quit guiding for a year and rodeoed hard. Sure enough, he'd won not only the bronc riding but the all-around title as well. His pickup had been a prize from that all-around title, given by one of the truck companies that sponsored a lot of the rodeos.

Everyone had liked John. He'd never had any enemies.

But there still might be some connection between his death and Jake's.

I took the address out of my chest pocket and looked at it again. There was no name, just an address. And it was in New Mexico.

George Wilkite 17

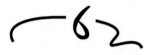

My last class had been on Friday morning, but with finals and projects to grade I wasn't able to leave for New Mexico as soon as I wanted. I spent most of the weekend grading. Partly because I wanted to finish this last task of the semester as early as possible so that I could leave. Partly because I wanted to keep my mind off Jake's death until the funeral on Monday.

A lot of the time was spent at my office at the college. No one was around over the weekend except for the janitors and a couple of administrators, so I was pretty much alone. I liked it that way.

Several times during the day, I'd stop the grading and just looked out the window. Outside, the weather hadn't turned horribly hot and sticky yet. The spring had brought an abundance of rains, and the campus was green with grass and trees. Sitting on a hilltop overlooking the town, the college lay on the opposite side of Interstate 35 from the bulk of the town. Just below the school, between it and the highway, a discount mall had sprung up. Bright signs hawking high-quality brand name outlets covered nearly twenty acres along the service road. It looked like three or four normal malls set end to end. At the intersection of the main exit and the highway, a convenience store/truck stop stayed crowded nearly twenty-four hours a day, seven days a week.

Sitting there looking out the window, I watched a pickup truck and horse trailer pull up to the gas pumps. It looked familiar, so I leaned forward in my seat, set my papers down, and watched to see if it was anyone I knew. There was writing on the trailer, but I couldn't make it out. As soon as the truck door opened and a set of long, smooth, muscular legs swung out, I began to smile. Chelsey Leskowitz, an old friend and three-time world champion in the Professional Women's Rodeo Association, was the only cowgirl with that particular set of legs.

As I watched, men spilled gas on their feet, stopped in mid-stride, or halted in the middle of the door opening to the convenience store as they noticed her. Sporting a pair of very short cut-off Wranglers, a tank top without a bra, tenny diggers, and a denim baseball cap, Chelsey almost got to the gas pump before the first male animal appeared and offered to pump the gas for her. I could imagine her sexy smile without even seeing it. She was a hand, all right. She'd smile and say something like, "Oh, would you?" and then grin to herself all the way to the store, knowing full well that her newfound, temporary servant was ogling the W's on her back pockets as she walked away from him.

Tired of grading, I dumped the whole batch of papers on my desk, locked the door, and sauntered down to the convenience store for a Dr Pepper. Chelsey spotted me coming across the parking lot, dropped the Boone's Farm Strawberry Hill bottles and the hot-to-go sandwiches on the counter, ran out the door, and just damn near leaped at me. Fortunately, her breasts cushioned the impact as she threw her arms around me and yelled, "IRA!"

It's a good thing I'm not inclined to embarrass easily. I returned Chelsey's hug and swung her around once. Despite Jake's death and the upcoming funeral, I felt a smile spread across my face. That's the effect Chelsey always had on me. We went back a long way—nearly ten years, when we'd both been wet-behind-the-ears rookies trying to fill our cards in the pros. We'd hooked up at a rodeo in Lake Charles, Louisiana, after an NIRA rodeo. She'd been going to Sam Houston State University and rode on the team there. I was from a little community college in South Texas. Somehow, we'd ended up as partners in a pool game after the rodeo. She broke and ran the table—three times. I didn't even get to shoot. When I finally did get to shoot, I at least didn't embarrass myself. We'd left the bar about $50 richer than we'd gone in, ended up at a Denny's, and stayed up all night talking. She was the most intelligent, most real person I had ever met. Under other circumstances, I'd have fallen smooth in love with Chelsey and probably asked her to marry me. I hadn't, but that's another story.

Pulling back from the kiss and hug, she looked up at me, smiled, and wiped lipstick off my face.

"What're you doin' here, Ira? I called your house this morning to let you know I was coming through, but I didn't get an answer."

"I been grading papers, girl. I, at least, still have to work for a living."

Back when I'd been working for Jake at the magazine, the Wrangler people had called asking about someone to endorse their jeans. I'd suggested Chelsey. They scoffed—until I sent them a picture of her. Most folks tend to expect cowgirls to be barrel racers. Chelsey wasn't. She team roped and ribbon roped, and she also rode bulls. When the Wrangler folks heard that, they figured she'd be some beat-up, tough-as-leather looking girl. She wasn't. They'd also balked because she wasn't a champion yet, until we showed them videos of her rides. She'd backed off on the rodeoing enough to miss the NIRA finals because she was doing a double major in business and veterinary science. Although she loved rodeo, she'd left college a full-blown vet with an accounting degree, one who knew how to make the money and how to make it grow. The endorsement came quick after they heard all that. Now she had her own vet clinic in West, Texas, just a few miles north of Waco.

She tucked a loose strand of blonde hair back up under the baseball cap. Stitched into the front of the cap in blazing orange and yellow were the words "Second Sucks!"

"Yeah, right. Cushy job at the college. And I was out pregnancy testing fifty cows this morning while you were sitting in the air conditioning, shuffling papers."

I looked hurt. "But they were heavy papers!"

We both laughed and she grabbed my arm and hustled me back into the store so she could pay for the gas and other items. Waiting for her change, she looked up at me.

"What you doin' tonight? I called to see if you wanted to go to Fort Worth with me. Since you weren't there, I left a sexy message on your machine."

"Sounds good. I need a break."

I looked at my watch. It was nearly 5:00 P.M. The drive to Northside Coliseum in Fort Worth took about an hour. Entry fees had to be paid by 7:30 P.M., a half hour before the performance started.

"Got time for me to run by the house, get a quick shower, and pick up my camera?"

"Sure," Chelsey said, snuggling up a little closer as we got to her truck. "Need me to help you wash your back?"

I noticed the hang-dog look on the face of Chelsey's latest temp-slave as we approached. He'd been hanging around, hoping to talk to her. She flashed him her patented smile and mouthed a sexy "Thank you" through those pouty lips of hers. He slunk off.

She grinned up at me, and I gave her a quick peck on the cheek.

"Let me get my truck from the campus and I'll meet you at my place," I said.

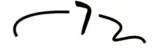

Chelsey busied herself checking on Spider, her roping horse, while I jumped into the shower and changed. Once I put on new jeans and a shirt, I pulled the camera case out from underneath the bed. I'd shot rodeo photos when I was competing to make up for those times I didn't win, and I'd been the photographer for the magazine when I worked for Jake. After I left the publication, I continued to shoot rodeo photos whenever I got the chance. Jake always bought them, and I kept my hand in the business and the sport.

I checked the equipment to make sure everything was charged and ready. I'd switched a few years back to the autofocus 35s with ultrasonic lenses simply because the only manual 35s anymore were at the top of the line. And in rodeo photography you don't want to use $1,000 camera bodies. It had taken some getting used to, but now I could focus on the action even faster than I had before.

I carried three main units and two backups. I'd never be able to afford that many if I'd depended on only photo sales to support it, but Jake had made a deal with the owner of the photo flash company and he had supplied me with free units in exchange for Jake putting the make of the flash under each of my photos. Norman, already preferred by rodeo photogs, had become the "official" *Texas Rodeo* magazine flash unit. After that, Jake had gone back to Canon and made the same deal with them. So I always had the best equipment. Even after I left, Jake kept me listed as the magazine's "official" photographer, which pretty much got me into any rodeo in the U.S. and guaranteed I stayed supplied with good equipment.

All the batteries were charged, so I put them back in the rodeo gear bag I used as a camera bag. Chelsey came into the house as I was packing up. She knew the routine. In the kitchen she took film out of the refrigerator and dumped it in the six-pack-size cooler. My cooler was white with a blue top and had a sticker that said "FILM" on each side so that I never mistook it for the medicine cooler Chelsey carried in her vet truck. Hers was exactly the same as mine, but it had a red top and a garish "BIO-HAZARD" sign on it. All of the gear went into the back of her 4x4 red Dodge Dually pickup.

I checked the mailbox and pulled out two bills, a copy of *Western Horseman,* and a letter from a Dallas law firm. I chunked the bills and letter back into the mailbox, grabbed the magazine, and we were off for Fort Worth.

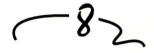

Chelsey drove. She would let me make the drive back after the rodeo. We'd been to enough shows together that she knew I tended to fall asleep during the heat of the afternoon but could stay awake all night long driving. On the other hand, she drove well during the day and tended to get sleepy on night drives. Move me to the passenger's seat during the afternoon, after I'd nearly dozed off at the wheel, and I'd be as alert and awake as if I'd just jumped out of bed in the morning. Same with Chelsey at night. We never questioned it, just figured somebody was looking out for both of us by pairing us on those trips.

We pulled into Northside Coliseum, also known as Cowtown Coliseum or more often as just plain Cowtown, at about 7:00 P.M. I unloaded Spider while Chelsey went and paid. She came back and began to saddle the black quarter horse. I pecked her on the cheek again, gathered up my camera equipment, and headed for the bucking chutes inside the coliseum while she began to warm Spider up.

Cowtown Coliseum had always been my favorite rodeo

arena in the entire world. Built in 1908, and the site of the world's first indoor rodeo in 1918, it had a sense of history that practically called out. You could almost hear the old-timers who had ridden there during the heyday of early rodeo. The coliseum had hosted Chief Quanah Parker and thirty-six of his Comanche braves in 1909 and, on the other end of the social spectrum, the Russian Ballet performed there in 1916 and the Chicago Grand Opera in 1919. Jess Willard fought an exhibition match there in 1918. Over the years, Teddy Roosevelt, Enrico Caruso, Bob Wills, Bob Hope, Doris Day, Elvis, and Jimmy Carter had appeared to Cowtown crowds.

And it was still going. Cowtown held a rodeo every Friday and Saturday night during the summer tourist season and hosted all sorts of special rodeos during the winter, including the PWRA Finals, where Chelsey had won her three world championships.

Once you're through the entrance tunnel and in the arena area, you really step back in time. The pen is small compared to modern arenas—perfect for bucking stock but sometimes a little crowded for team roping. Headers barely have time to turn steers before they run into the opposite fence. It always reminded me of the old high school gyms in rural towns in Texas and Oklahoma I frequented when I worked as a newspaper photographer. But it had character. During the winter, the wind howled outside and sometimes inside, and in a deluge water drops would fly through little gaps between the glass panes that formed a band down both sides of the coliseum. Like old-time arenas, it still had a bandstand to one side of the announcer's platform above the bucking chutes, and most of the finals still featured a live rodeo band. Tonight there was just an announcer, a secretary, and a timer above the chutes, the announcer's sound system and a stack of labeled tapes next to it taking the place of the band.

Behind the bucking chutes, a little knot of five or six

cowboys were tying cinches onto their bareback riggings with latigoes. One of them was Monk Adams, the fellow bareback rider from my Madison Square Garden picture. Monk was showing a younger cowboy how to tie off his rigging properly, running the latigo back through the last loop of leather, then pulling it tight.

"And then, on a horse, you'd run it up under the front of your riggin' and through the dee on the other side," he told him, referring to the large steel D-ring that was used to tie the rigging to a bronc.

I goosed Monk and he jumped—a little too exagerated—and turned on me with his pocketknife pulled as if he were going to cut me. But there was a big grin on his face.

"Seen me coming, huh?" I asked, grinning back.

"Yep," he said, brandishing the knife about ear-high. "If I hadn't seen ya, I'd have probably been cutting cockleburs out o' your mane."

He pocketed the knife and clapped me on the shoulder.

"Tell this boy I ain't bullshittin' about the single tie on the latigo," he said, pointing at the young bareback rider, probably eighteen or so, who studied the rigging with some concern. He stopped long enough to look up at me with questions all over his face.

"Monk's right, son. It'll hold. Watch some of the other hands tonight and see how they do it. It's quicker to re-pull if you need to for some reason, and the hands in the deriggin' chute will like you a lot better."

My confirmation seemed to settle his fears, so Monk and I ambled off toward the concession stand for a Dr Pepper before the rodeo started. I paid for them and handed Monk his as we worked our way back toward the chutes.

"You entered tonight, ol' pard?" I asked.

Monk nodded his head while sipping his DP, then swallowed.

"Yeah, they ain't been getting the best bronc riders here the last few weeks, so I figured I ought to take some of their money. Was up in Mesquite last night. I'm winning a second and hope it'll hold up. Beat Claudie Schaeffer by about ten points, the son of a bitch."

We both laughed. Claudie Schaeffer wasn't much liked. He was about as dishonest as they come and would probably cheat his own mother. Besides that, he was plumb obnoxious, and we all reveled in beating his butt whenever we got the chance.

"He come through with a bunch of pretty good kids he's hauling around. They was headed for the West Coast and was trying to pick up some easy money from the permit holders. But me and Snake was there. Snake's winning it. Went 74 on Bent Creek last night. Damn, that bitch bucked!"

Snake was Eric Copperhead. He was about our age and had ridden with us a couple of years before Monk and I started to slow down. Bent Creek was a new mare that Neal Gay had bought at the Miles City Bucking Horse Sale the year before and named her for the Canadian town she'd come from. She was half draft horse and half quarter horse and had feet the size of dinner plates. Riding her was like having your hand tied to a freight train engine when it fell off a cliff. She could jerk a cowboy down before he even knew she'd started dropping to the ground. She wasn't anything showy; she just damn near tore your arm off every jump until the whistle.

I chatted with Monk until the rest of the cowboys started drifting in, then turned to business. I took orders from each of the three young riders I didn't know, got their names and addresses, and said hi to the four other cowboys I knew. We all knew each other well enough that I'd just send them any good pictures I got and they'd send the money back. If I got one that was bad, I wouldn't bother. If it was debatable, I'd wait and show them a proof next time I saw them and see if they wanted it.

The grand entry started, and I saw Chelsey ride in on

Spider. She glanced over at me and Monk standing on the slats of the chutes and threw me a pursed-lip kiss, then she wiggled fingers at Monk and rode on.

"Damn, Ira, that lady horse doctor still after you?"

"Hell, Monk, she ain't after me. We're just good friends."

"Yeah, right! I wish I had lady friends like that."

We took off our hats for the national anthem and the invocation, and then I headed out in front of the chutes to shoot pictures and Monk started pulling riggings.

I got a good one of Monk on his ride and a couple of the other good hands there. Two of the top cowboys had bad luck. One's horse turned over on him in the chute, and he was hauled away unconscious—a concussion, we later found out. The other one's horse ran halfway down the arena before it started bucking, too late for me to get a picture but just early enough to keep him from getting a reride. All three young cowboys got thrown off in or near the gate. Monk won it with a 71.

I got a good shot of Chelsey and her team roping partner, Angie Blake, making a good run. They split second and third. They were the only females in the male-dominated event, even though most of the team ropers I know have a wife, girlfriend, or sister who helps them practice when other guys aren't around. Some of them are good enough to compete. Angie and Chelsey had finally said to hell with it and started entering traditional rodeos in the team roping in addition to the PWRA events.

The bull riding was good for pictures, eight good shots out of ten. With orders from the other events, I'd grossed $300 for the night, 12 bucks more than Monk won and about twice what Chelsey picked up for her share of the second-third split. They collected their winnings and, armed with cash, we headed into the Cowtown night.

First place we landed was right across Exchange Street at the White Elephant Saloon. The White Elephant has been there forever, it seems. It wasn't the Longbranch Saloon out of *Gunsmoke,* but it was pretty close. Dark-paneled wood walls reflected golden-yellow lamplight, giving the bar a nice, warm, homey look. Twenty years ago it had been a died-in-the-wool cowboy hangout, the only regulars being contestants from the rodeo across the street and a few old cowboys or up-and-coming hands who lived in the area. It gradually began to be frequented by suits, both male and female, from the downtown office crowd or, even worse, from Dallas. Those folks, as well as tourists, were keeping the place alive now.

As we stepped through the doors, the little three-piece country-and-western band took a break and the lights came up a bit. No sooner did they leave the stage than a drunken young secretary-type sprang onto the stage from where she had been sitting at a nearby table. Clad in too-new jeans and an unshaped cowboy hat, it was obvious she and her other three female companions had come to the "bad" side of town for a little risky entertainment. By this time, she had become well acquainted with Jose Cuervo and wanted a little more excitement than the occasional dance with the real or wannabe cowboys in the place.

She put a dollar in the jukebox on the stage and hit a button, leaning on the brightly lit music machine until the music started. Monk and I waved at Coot, the bartender, and leaned our backs against the bar waiting for him to get down our way. Chelsey just sort of melted into me, all warm and soft, and Monk gave me that knowing sideways look of his as if to say, "Yeah, right. Friends!" At about the time our backs hit the bar, the music started on the stage and Little Miss Secretary Sue turned around and looked straight at us, mostly at Monk.

"Wild Thing" boomed out of the speakers and, in rhythm with the music, Secretary Sue started slinking toward the front of the stage, one booted foot sliding provocatively in front of the other and exaggerating the swing of her very nice, denim-clad hips. Without ever taking her eyes from Monk's, she slunk toward him as far as the stage would allow, then turned slowly and sensuously, only to flip her hair and look over her shoulder at him while she reached up with her hands to her blouse. I knew what it looked like she was going to do, but I figured I'd wait and see.

Sure enough, her hands were busy while her back was to us and, when she turned around, there wasn't a button in place on her blouse. She pulled it aside in a way that allowed Monk and us to see her black-laced breasts but kept them from view of the rest of the patrons. But that kind of behavior doesn't escape the notice of cowboys, drunks, and bartenders for long. A couple of hooting calls came from one side of the bar as she dropped her blouse on the floor behind her and reached for the front snap on her bra.

George Wilhite 31

Behind me I heard Coot holler something but couldn't turn around to look. My eyes were riveted to the two large, probably surgically enhanced breasts as they popped free of the black lace. Her nipples were as big as pencil erasers and stood straight out.

"Hell, and it ain't even cold in here," Monk muttered from beside me as he started to sip the beer Coot had brought him. "She must just be excited to see a real cowboy in here amongst all these panty-waists."

The black lace bra came flying straight at Monk, draping itself over the Coors longneck and hiding his big handlebar mustache behind a black film. He never missed a swallow, then reached up, grabbed the bra in one big paw, raised it to his nose, and sniffed.

"Damn, and she smells nice, too."

With that, he pushed off the bar, crossed the ten feet to the stage, and despite catcalls from the rest of the residents of the White Elephant, grabbed the girl around the waist and lifted her bodily from the stage. He was carrying her one-handed back to the bar when a Fort Worth policeman came storming in, looking at him and the topless young lady, then at Coot.

Monk winked at Coot.

"I can handle this for ya, Coot, if you don't want to make no fuss about it," he said, nodding at the cop and then moving his eyes to include the three friends of the girl who were still drinking and paying no attention whatsoever to their friend.

Coot mentally tallied up lost profits, shook his head at the cop, and went back to waiting customers. The cop picked up the girl's blouse from the stage and handed it to Monk.

"Make sure she gets this back on, then," he said before turning on his heel and walking out. If this was the worst thing he ran into tonight, he'd be more than happy to let Monk take care of it for him.

Monk carried the girl to us, her breasts staring me and Chelsey right in the face.

"Tip my hat, girl, and say goodbye to the nice folks," Monk said.

She reached up to Monk's black felt Resistol and gently tipped the brim.

"Goodbye, y'all," she said.

Monk grinned real big then and started out the door.

"Make sure you put that blouse on, girl," Monk said. "The nice policeman asked you to."

She pouted. "But won't that be a waste of time?" she asked, her red lips making more of a frown.

Monk appeared to think for a moment. "You're right. To hell with it."

The blouse went flying into the air as he carried her out the door and onto the street. The last we saw, the pair was headed toward the contestant parking lot, leaving a trail of astonished tourists in their wake and a bewildered gray-haired couple from Ohio wondering where the blue satin blouse that landed on the man's head had come from.

After Monk left, Chelsey and I had a couple of beers and danced a few slow ones. Pretty soon we got hungry and headed to the steakhouse around the corner. An hour and two good sirloins later, we found ourselves alone on a balcony behind the steakhouse overlooking the concrete creek that runs behind the saloons and dancehalls around the coliseum.

We sat close, side by side, but each of us was lost in our own separate world. I was thinking about Jake, and she was thinking about something. I didn't know what. Until she finally spoke.

"I heard about Jake, Ira," she said softly as she took a sip of a whiskey sour. "I'm sorry."

I was drinking ice water now since I had to drive back, but it gave me an excuse to catch my thoughts. I wasn't real good with this emotional stuff, so I did what I usually did—I made a wisecrack.

"Oh, and here I thought you invited me for a night out on the town because of my manly good looks and witty chatter."

She turned toward me in the low glow of white Christmas lights that hung all around the balcony railing and in the branches of a couple of stunted fig-looking trees that rose from the concrete waterway. My wisecrack never even fazed her. She knew me too well.

"Well, there's always that, too. But this morning was the first chance I had to call you. I didn't even hear about it until this morning. The rancher whose cows I was pregnancy testing knows one of the EMTs who took Jake and you to the hospital. The EMT had come to help him work the cattle that morning."

"Must've been Bucky," I interrupted, thankful for some tangent to go off on. "His wife's dad has cattle. You must have been at Mr. Tyler's ranch."

She nodded and sipped her drink. Neither of us said anything for a minute, but I could feel her looking at me.

"You never break, do you?"

I looked over and met her eyes. At that moment, I noticed how pretty and green they were. I almost said something we'd avoided for years, something that we both knew, something that I wasn't free to say.

"Yeah, I break sometimes. But not when it has to do with Jake. He always said to get your work done first, then you got time to do whatever needs being done, whether that's party time or breaking-down time."

She turned away from me then and I thought I heard a sniffle, but I couldn't be sure. Then she turned back to me.

"When's the funeral?"

It was my turn to look away.

"Monday. Ten in the morning."

"Want some company?"

Our eyes met again, both of us sad. I knew why I was, and I thought I knew why she was, but I let it go.

"I'd love some company, Chelsey. I really would. I sometimes think I'm getting to be just a damned old hardcase. I appreciate the offer."

With a twist of her head, she laughed it off and stood up in front of me, hands out.

"Well, Mr. Hardcase, it's Saturday night in Cowtown and I believe you owe me some more dancing."

I eased up out of the chair and took her hands in mine. A twinge went through me as I knew this was a perfect chance to say what I wanted to say to her, but I couldn't at this point in my life.

"You're right," I said, "I think I hear Billy Bob's calling our name."

Pulling her close to me, I marveled at the feel and smell of her. She started doing schottische and Cotton-Eyed Joe steps along the sidewalk as we headed toward the world's biggest honky-tonk. I held her right hand as she twirled to the only two line dances any self-respecting cowboy I know would do. As she ended the twirl and slid back in step with me, she grabbed my waist and looked up into my eyes, smiling.

"Manly good looks, witty chatter, and not a bad dancer, too. I'm impressed."

I laughed. "Hell, woman, you quit being impressed with me years ago."

Her eyes twinkled in the streetlights. "Just get me to Billy Bob's *quick* . . . I need a dancing fix."

The day of the funeral, I picked Chelsey up at her office. We were both in jeans and hats. We'd both known better than to dress up fancy for Jake's funeral. It just wasn't his way. A few folks from the other horse magazines were supposed to be coming, some old champs had called to say they would be there, and the field editors were trying to make it back from their respective rodeos. Other than that, it was probably only going to be Chelsey and me.

There wasn't going to be a church service as such. Jake had never been much of one for churches. In fact, he'd been a cantankerous old cuss who'd done things his way and didn't really care what other people—especially holier-than-thou types—thought about him or his activities. Consequently, I'd opted for a service in a local cemetery where his parents had been buried. In line with his wishes, I'd had him cremated and asked the mortician for a small bag of ashes to be set aside for me. He had them waiting at the graveside when we arrived.

There had been enough room in his parents' little burial plot for another grave. When I went to make arrangements, I found he'd paid for the whole plot when he'd buried his folks, nearly thirty years before.

The plot sat in the shade of a huge, split-trunk hackberry tree that was one of a line of hackberries that had probably sprouted along a fence line that disappeared long ago. Farmers and ranchers in the area were familiar with such lines of hackberries. Birds would eat the berries, then go sit on a nearby fence to deposit the seeds in their droppings. Such indiscriminate toilet habits produced lines of hackberries that grew up through fences all over Central Texas, often growing around the wires. Evidence of this activity existed in the cemetery's line of hackberries in the form of short pieces of rusted barbed wire that protruded from almost every tree. But the gravesite was shady and cool, even in the middle of a warm Texas spring morning.

Under the green canvas awning with "Lawton's Funeral Home" screenprinted on the edge, only four men were waiting. One was the pastor, Brother Blake Martinez, of a tiny Czech-Polish-German church in Leroy, between West and Waco. Brother Blake, as he always introduced himself, pronounced his name the Czech way, Martin-Yetz. His church was the church Jake's father and mother had attended. He was a nice man, very intent on his job, but he'd never seen Jake in his church. His predecessor, Vaslav Sefcik, now ninety-two, still lived in the parsonage of the church while Brother Blake, his wife, and two young children had moved into a house in West. Brother Sefcik was one of the other men there, his slight frame resting in the front row of the ten or twelve chairs, beside Brother Blake.

A few chairs over to one side sat two men in local rancher attire—khaki pants over low-heeled Roper boots, white long-sleeved sports shirts with pinstripe from Wal-Mart or Bill's Dollar Store, clip-on ties (one maroon, one navy), sports coats from some unknown source (one maroon, one navy), and straw hats from the local hardware store or Tractor Supply Company. Each had a memo pad, probably covered in livestock prices from the Waco or West auction, and a couple of pens stashed in his breast pocket. The sports coat lapels couldn't quite cover the bulk of paper and pens, so they peeked out from underneath the too-small jackets. Even before they turned their heads, I recognized them.

Tommy "Hooks" Adwell had been a bull rider from Jake's era. He now ran a little spread east of I-35, the interstate that divided Texas into East and West Texas. To the east, the land was blackland, occasional sand, some sandy loam or red clay. Most of it was good, productive crop or pastureland.

Next to Hooks, former saddle bronc rider Danny "Stripes" Owens was nodding his head and checking the backs of his hands and his fingernails while Adwell talked in polite whispers. Owens owned a place just west of I-35, in the limestone-and-cedar country that marked the beginning of West Texas. Stripes had won the saddle bronc championship the same year Jake had won the bull riding title.

I nodded and shook hands with the two pastors, then stepped across to shake hands with the two old-timers. I knew them well enough from their stops by the office to drink coffee and talk with Jake. Between the three of us, we exchanged few words, mainly in my introduction of Chelsey, who'd already done quite a bit of vet work for each of them. We sat down beside the old cowboys and I nodded to Brother Blake to start.

Brother Blake introduced himself and Brother Sefcik briefly, then began his eulogy.

"I'm speaking for Brother Vaslav today because he was the pastor to Jake Lawson's mother and father. When he heard of Jake's death, he wanted to come himself, despite his advanced years. I agreed to accompany him and speak for him."

Brother Blake leaned down to listen to a few mumbled words from his elder, then straightened and resumed his speech.

"Brother Vaslav says that he was the pastor when Jake was born. He says his mother and father were so happy to have a healthy baby boy."

The two pastors did the leaning, mumbling thing again before Brother Blake spoke another couple of sentences. It went on like that for about fifteen minutes. Apparently, the old pastor remembered Jake as a small child still, and he said little that related to the man we had known. Still, it was nice to hear that the old man considered Jake to be honest and well-meaning. He stopped short of saying that he would go to heaven.

Finally, I spread the reserved ashes over the gravesite. We all walked out from under the awning after shaking hands with the pastors and thanking them for coming. In the background, I saw the funeral director pull up in a pickup with a trailer. Two men got out and started toward the gravesite, stopping at the treeline to sit and take out smokes, apparently waiting as inconspicuously as possible for us to finish so they could take down the tent and load up the chairs.

We walked silently to my truck, which was parked behind the two battered old pickups of the ranchers. Leaning on the bedrail, the old-timers pulled out cigarettes and lit up. Adwell blew a ring of smoke, then another smaller one through it, and watched the two circles float away on the breeze. Then he turned and looked squarely into my eyes.

"Son, I got an ol' .45-70 Marlin in the back window of the pickup there," he said, pointing with his head to the truck in front of mine. "You find out who done this, all you got to do is call and I'll blow a hole the size of a softball in that son-of-a-bitch's gut and stand there and pour salt into it until he dies."

He finished the cigarette, dropped the butt to the ground, and ground it in hard with his boot heel before looking back up at me. His eyes met mine, and there was no mercy in them.

"And I got a lot of time and a lot of salt."

The old rancher didn't shake hands or say goodbye. He just left, moving slow and stiff, even in the warm sunshine of the Texas morning.

Owens took his place in front of me.

"That goes for me, too," he said, his gaze never flinching. "And we ain't bullshittin'. You need help, son, you holler." He stopped long enough to tip his TSC hat toward Chelsey. "Ma'am."

Then we were alone.

12

I'd been sitting in the little café across from the post office in Espanola for two days—breakfast, lunch, and dinner. I'd finished my grading the Sunday before Jake's funeral. After I'd dropped the grades and papers off at the English Department office Monday afternoon, I'd loaded the truck and headed for New Mexico. I hadn't even known where Espanola was when I'd left Texas. Fortunately, it was big enough to show up on the map, just northwest of Santa Fe. Situated in the middle of two Indian reservations, a national forest, and a wilderness area, the town had a population that was mostly Indian and Mexican, and it laid claim to being the Low Rider Capital of the World. For two days, I'd seen mainly pickups and low riders pass in front of the café.

I sat at a corner table near where the café wall and the front window met. The café had once been an old variety store, and the front display window stretched from a couple of feet above the floor all the way to the ceiling. The corner table was conveniently obscured from the street by the glare from the sun-drenched street on the huge glass windows and the shadows of the dimly lit interior. The inside was nearly vacant, with a handful of mismatched tables and appropriately mismatched chairs in the front third of the building. A wall cut across half of the store to separate the kitchen area from the front. Through the tunnel-like opening between the kitchen and the far side wall, I had seen pool tables, their beer lights off the first morning I'd come in. Locals started dropping in around 4:00 or so each afternoon to drink a little beer and shoot pool.

From my table I glanced toward the post office while I picked at my food. The first day, I had taken so long over each meal that the owner, named Felipe, had kept an anxious eye on me. I finally explained that I was a stockbroker from Dallas, suffering from stress, and was here on doctor's orders to rest. Unfortunately, he played the penny stocks and asked for some advice. I had to let him feed me the names, because I didn't know a stock from a plate of eggs. But he'd been more than happy to tell me what he had and what he was thinking of buying and even happier to take the nods and shakes of my head as sage advice. When he brought me my eggs and tortillas the second day, he was grinning. He had owned one of the stocks I'd shaken my head at and had sold it immediately. Overnight, it had dropped drastically. Apparently, I had saved him more than $300. My meals were free that day.

I had just come in for lunch, slightly before 11:00 A.M., and Felipe was still grinning at me when I saw a familiar face head into the post office. It reappeared in less than a minute and headed straight for the café. John Davis, former world champion and looking none the worse for being dead for nearly three years, spotted me and walked over like nothing had ever happened.

"Howdy, Ira," he said, flipping an opened letter to me. "I got your letter."

My first day in Espanola, I'd mailed a letter to the address Jake had given me, with only the initials J.D. for a name. It said:

John:
If you're alive, I'll be in the café across the street at mealtimes.

Ira Carter

I looked at the note, then back up at John Davis. "So, I take it you are alive, then."

13

J.D. laughed as he sat down across the table from me. I motioned to Felipe for another cup of coffee.

"Yeah, for the moment. But I wouldn't be for long if anyone else knew I was here. I take it Jake sent you? I thought he might be getting a little old for this kind of stuff."

"Sort of. Jake's dead, J.D."

The smile faded on his face and he shook his head slowly from side to side.

"I told him to let it lie." He looked up at me with sadness in his eyes. "He was a good man, Ira. Best I've ever known."

"Yeah," I said, looking away, "he was. Like a father to me."

"So, did he send you or not?"

I looked back at J.D. and noticed that his jaw was set, his stare wary. He looked much the same as he had three years ago, but you'd have to know him to recognize him now. He had cut off what we used to call a Wild West mustache—one of those that came all the way down past his lips and fluttered slightly whenever he said certain words. He'd been out in the sun even more than before and was weathered a deep, dark brown. His high cheekbones were still there, but his prominent hawk-nose had been broken or changed surgically, I couldn't tell which. He had adopted the "rez" dress of the local Navajo men, mostly cowboy shirt and Wranglers, but with lace-up boots instead of regular cowboy boots. He'd added an exquisitely crafted silver concho belt and an old, open-crowned, flat-brimmed black felt. You couldn't see the world champion cowboy for the stereotypical Indian front that J.D. had taken on.

Felipe showed up with the mug and set it down in front of J.D., nodding at him in recognition. J.D. nodded back in silence, taking his eye off me just long enough to acknowledge the owner. I waited until Felipe went back into the kitchen, his gray head visible through the order window cut into the wall, before I said anything.

"He handed me your address as he was dying. He never said anything except 'find him' before he died."

"That's good enough for me, if it is for you. So, you in on this deal or not?" His gaze was still unflinching.

"J.D., I don't even know what's going on. What the hell is happening? You're supposed to be murdered, Jake has been murdered, and I don't know why."

J.D. looked hard into my eyes for several seconds, then nodded. "The one thing Jake always said about you was that you could be counted on to do right. Said it sometimes got you into trouble. I guess I have to agree with him. So I'll tell you what's going on with one condition: if you think it's right, you're involved; if not, you promise not to say anything to anyone else about this whole deal and I'll let it lie too and go back to sleeping with both eyes closed at night. Deal?"

I reached across the table and took his outstretched hand. He shook it firmly, let go, then let his gaze drift down to the table. He took a sip of his coffee before he started. So did I.

"It's the Mafia, Ira. They're in the sport."

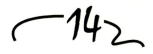

I nearly choked on the coffee I'd swallowed. He held up a hand and nodded his head to stop my question.

"I know. It's hard to believe. But they've been around for a while. Did Jake ever tell you who he rode with in the fifties?"

"Sure. Al Abbey, Gavin Blake, Red Schoefield, Andy Tetracini . . ."

"Andy Tetracini. Did he ever tell you who he was?"

"Yeah, I knew Andy real well when I worked at the magazine. But back then he was just some guy from New York who wanted to be a cowboy, so he moved down to Texas, living on his folks' money, and tried to rodeo. He was okay but not good enough to make a living at it."

"And did Jake say what ever happened to him?"

"Sure. He said he quit after a few years and moved back to New York. They used to keep in touch and every now and then do favors for each other. When we were looking for new camera equipment . . . Wait a minute, he joked then that Andy was in the mob and could get him anything he wanted. But that was just a joke. He said so—said later that Andy was an importer and one of the things he imported was cameras. Jake said he could get us our equipment at wholesale."

J.D. shook his head. "He wasn't joking, Ira. Andy is a don in the Mafia in New York. He probably did get the equipment for you at wholesale, maybe even less. He has a hand in almost everything."

"But that wouldn't have gotten Jake killed. He's known about that for forty years or more."

"Right. Jake was killed because he knew where I was. I know about how they operate in the sport. I used to work for them, but I quit. It was no big deal until I won the world. Then they wanted me to start back again. I couldn't. I had a family by then. I didn't want them involved."

"Whoa, there, J.D. What do you mean you worked for them? You were from Oklahoma. How could you get mixed up in that?"

"When I rodeoed, before I met Linda, I was single and wild. I spent a lot of money partying. One night I got into a card game after the Madison Square Garden rodeo. They knew I'd won and let me play on the check I had coming. But the check was only for $1,200. I lost nearly $3,000. When I couldn't pay it all, they made me a deal. I would drive a brand new white Cadillac that would be parked in the hotel parking lot back to Oklahoma for them, stop in Oklahoma City for the night, park the car in the hotel parking lot, and spend the night. They'd give me spending money so I could party and the next morning I could drive the car on home. It was mine. All I had to do was occasionally spend certain nights in certain hotels around the country. They would make sure that those nights coincided with rodeos I was entered in. Every now and then, I would get a call saying I should enter a certain rodeo. I always did. I also always won that rodeo unless I got bucked off or just really blew the ride."

"What was with the cars?"

"When I got in the car the next morning, it was a different one. Oh, it was a white Cadillac, exactly like the one I'd driven in. Even had the same license plate number and the same Vehicle Identification Number. But it was different. One night on my way to St. Louis for one of my required rodeos, I dropped a cigarette on the upholstery. Put a scar on the leather. The next morning, there was no scar. Everything from my old car was in the new one—sunglasses, ticket stubs, empty cigarette packages, everything. But the car was different. After that, I started putting little ID marks on the cars somewhere inconspicuous. Maybe a piece of electrician's tape on a wire under the dash. Or a scratch on a fender. Every night I stayed at a hotel, I drove away in a different car."

"Do you know what was in them? Drugs? What?"

"They told me that it was only money that I was transporting across state lines, headed for Vegas to be laundered. But I found out different."

"How?"

"I had been given a number to call in case of an accident. One night I hit a black Angus bull between Oklahoma City and Dallas. Killed him and totaled the car. There was a car phone in the car. I called the number. A voice said they'd have someone right out. I got out of the car and started walking around, looking at the damage and trying to clear my head. From inside one of the fenders, a white powder started sifting out. The whole damn car was loaded with cocaine."

J.D. looked away from me for a second, the little muscle just below that high right cheekbone of his tightening and loosening. When he turned back toward me, his eyes were cold again and there was a deep, dark edge to his voice.

"That was when I quit. I told Andy that hauling money was one thing, but I wouldn't haul their drugs for them.

He was all nice about it. Said okay. But his son didn't like it a bit. Said I knew too much. You know his son, don't you? Frankie Armstrong?"

"Armstrong? The short little bull rider from New York? He's Andy's son? He rodeos all the time. When would he have the time to run any mob business? And what about his name?"

"He took his mother's name—thought it was more 'cowboy' sounding. And he runs the business the way all the big-time cowboys run theirs—by cellular phone, laptop, and fax. Andy was a gentleman about letting me out, saying I'd done more than my share for an outsider, that the cocaine had been a mistake. He said I should have been hauling money only. We shook hands. No hard feelings.

"But when I was closing in on the world title, I got a call from Frankie. He wanted me to do some jobs for them. He had been the one who switched the cash for the cocaine on my last run. Said he had big plans for me once I had the world title under my belt. Something about a line of rodeo equipment with my name on it and shipping coke out in the rosin bags. Thought the cops might be interested in my 'drug-running past,' as he called it. Said it would be a disaster for me but that there was no way to trace it to him. He wouldn't take no for an answer. In between, I'd met Linda and we'd gotten married. We had two boys. I wasn't about to get them involved in it. I went ahead and won the world, but then I 'killed' myself."

"And Jake found out you were still alive?"

"Yeah, he was going to do an exposé on the mob in rodeo. He thought they had killed me. That was what made him decide to do the story. He let everything drop, even the magazine, while he compiled a file on it. Then he found out I was alive."

"But how? Everyone was convinced you were dead. Even your wife and kids."

"It had to be that way. If they had been acting, some-one would have noticed. Those guys can find anyone once they decide to. They even have contacts here. Fortunately, they didn't really believe that I was alive still."

"But how did they find out?"

"One of the field editors is with the mob. I know which one. I may be the only one who does. He saw a copy of Jake's article in the office one day. He also saw part of my letter to Jake, with only my initials, so they're not sure it was me. He didn't see the address, though. Jake kept it somewhere else. He also burned the letter after that. I told him to forget the article, to let sleeping dogs lie, that it was too dangerous. But he said if anything looked out of the ordinary, he'd get in touch with you. He thought a lot of you."

"But why did you get in touch with Jake in the first place? You were safe. No one knew where you were. You would have never been found, even by me, if that address didn't exist."

"You said Jake was like a father to you. Well, he *was* my father."

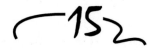

As J.D. and I rode out to his place on the reservation, he filled me in.

"My mother was one of those *la-ti-da* Eastern ladies that Jake met when he was at Madison Square Garden. The Garden lasted about a month back then, and Jake made a big impression on my mother. I think he won the bull riding, bronc riding, and placed in the steer wrestling. She was young and didn't see eye-to-eye with her folks then. Ran off with Jake more to piss them off than because she loved him, I think. Now, don't get me wrong. She loved him, but she and her folks were really at odds. Always were.

"Anyway, they got hitched in Philadelphia on the way out of town. For a couple of years, everything was okay, but then she got pregnant with me. She wanted to settle down, but he didn't. So they compromised. He started the magazine and cut back on his rodeoing. Unfortunately, the magazine took as much traveling as the rodeoing did, so he was gone a lot."

He looked toward me then, but I couldn't distinguish

his face much since we were passing through the shadow of a mesa that cut off the light from a dying sunset. Then he turned on the lights and the green glow of the dash lights allowed me to see the tight line of his lips as he looked back at the road and continued.

"Well, it was more than she could take, being alone there all the time. We were living on his place down by the river, in that old two-room sharecropper's house that used to be there."

I remembered it. It was maybe ten feet wide, twenty long. He used it as a feed shed when I worked for him. There was a hole where the fireplace had stood on one end of it patched with old plywood. The house had burned down years ago when a high school couple used it for a lover's nest. Joke was that their passion had caught the hay on fire. Actually, a little kerosene heater they'd brought with them caused the fire. Things had gotten passionate, the boy had finally admitted to police, and they'd knocked the heater over, spilling kerosene over everything. I'd wondered at the time why Jake got so upset about it. There wasn't more than $200 worth of feed and hay in it, and he'd been doing good then, so it wasn't that much of an economic setback to him. He'd been talking about building a newer, more modern hay barn for years.

"One night, my mom got me out of bed, threw all our clothes in a suitcase, and took some of the ad money that had come in for the magazine. We caught a train for back East that night. Mom had only taken enough for our fare, so we rode all the way to New York without anything to eat. I was maybe two or three.

"When we got to New York, I was amazed. Mom's folks had money. We caught a cab to their house, and when it pulled up there I thought I was at a castle. It was huge. She didn't have the money to pay the cab fare, so the cabbie made me stay in the car until she came back with it.

Her parents weren't in, so she had to beg the money off one of the servants."

J.D. looked over at me long enough to grin real big before switching his attention back to the curving road that ran alongside the Rio Grande.

"His name was Rutherford. He was this big, old butler who never smiled when Mom or her folks were around. He was like one of those guards at Buckingham Palace that never changes expression. He was hesitant to give my mother the money until she brought him out to the cab to see me. I'd been crying because I was cold and hungry— it was just before Christmas—and old Rutherford took one look at me and handed the cabbie the fare. Then he turned, real stiff-like, the way those English butlers do, and asked my mom when I had last eaten. She told him we'd been on the train two days without food. He turned back to me in the cab, reached out two giant hands, and said, 'Let's get the little fellow something to eat.' Neither Mom nor I had a coat, and when he picked me up, I wanted to snuggle down in those big warm arms forever."

J.D. stopped talking for a minute and shook his head slightly before continuing.

"I'll never forget that man. He woke up every servant in the house. Made them make a complete meal just for the two of us. I sat on his lap the whole time and ate and ate and ate. He laughed at me a lot, saying that I was going to get so fat my belly button would pop right off. I must have gotten scared of that happening, because I remember his face going from laughing to concerned as he comforted me that he was just joking. Then he held me in his arms and sang to me, an old English lullaby he said. I drifted off to sleep right there."

J.D.'s head dropped for a second and he gave a little sigh.

"Anyway, to make a long story short, we lived there until I was sixteen. That's when I found out about the letter Mom's dad sent Jake."

I didn't need to see J.D.'s face to know he was getting mad. He pounded the steering wheel hard enough to shake the pickup.

"The ol' son-of-a-bitch wrote Dad telling him Mother and I had boarded the train for New York but had died from the exposure we suffered at the sharecropper's shack while he was gone. Told him not to bother to come back East for the funeral, that he'd make sure he couldn't attend. Even threatened him with a lawsuit. They had told me about Dad, but only that he'd been a rancher and a rodeo cowboy who'd died soon after I was born. That was all I knew about him. There may have been some truth to their lie, I guess. Mom died when I was four. Effects of exposure on my dad's ranch, my grandparents said. Rutherford said it was alcohol. Drunk herself to death one night. He said she had still loved my father, but my grandparents wouldn't have anything to do with him. They fought. She cried. They went out for the evening. She sat on the couch, he said, and finished off a fifth of vodka. Trouble was, she never drank. It was too much for her, he said, and it killed her. He blamed my grandparents. I did, too, after I found the letter."

J.D.'s anger had been replaced by sadness. His eyes blinked rapidly to keep from tearing up. Then, with a single sniff, he became the same flippant, devil-may-care cowboy I had always known.

"So, one day I just walked out of the house. It was just after my birthday, and all those rich relatives had given me enough money for presents that I was able to fly down to Texas to find Jake. Walked in on him while he was putting out the magazine. Took me a good hour to convince him I was really his son. But finally I did.

"He decided that his house would be the first place they'd look, so he took me out to his father's place. Big man, half Swede and half German. Worked a couple hundred acres of cotton in the Brazos River bottom. He was seventy or more when I came. My grandmother was a little woman, full Comanche. Made beaded pieces and did beautiful leatherwork. Taught me how to do it, too. She was maybe sixty or so then. They raised me until I was eighteen. Dad quit hitting the road and came out every day after work. You know him—that would be 7:00 or 8:00 P.M. most nights. But we'd sit and talk out there on a little warped wooden porch in the middle of all those acres of white cotton bolls. He missed my mom a lot. Said he wished he'd have done better by her, but that rodeo was all he'd ever known and that the magazine was the only way he'd known to try to settle down and make some money. He guessed she hadn't realized the only reason he'd stayed on the road with the magazine was to try to make a go of it so he'd be able to get off the road eventually.

"Anyway, we decided I should keep my Mom's maiden name. Her dad had it changed when we moved to New York. The less people knew, the less they could tell anybody. At eighteen, I started rodeoing."

Linda welcomed me like a long lost brother. The two boys had grown since I'd last seen them—at their dad's funeral. They were both stronger, bigger, and tanner than before. John, Jr. was nearly six and his brother, Zack, had just turned four. They shook hands like men and kept quiet while their dad and I talked about what was to come.

J.D. was determined to find the person who had killed his father. He didn't think it was Andy, but he certainly couldn't prove it without putting his family in danger. I knew he wasn't concerned for his own life. He never had been. I'd seen him go in on a fighting bull to get a cowboy off after the clown had been knocked out. He'd taken a horn in the side (in fact, he still carried the scar), but he got the cowboy out of there. The horn punctured a lung and bruised his heart, and he almost died. But after several months in the hospital, he was soon riding again. That year, he decided to go for the world title.

J.D. knew of a place where the mob had a hideaway in the Hill Country of Texas west of Austin. To the locals there, it was the corporate retreat of a major East Coast firm. But it had been built by the mob before there were even roads in that area. Just after World War II, they had cleared a rough road into the area to allow their contractors to build a private runway and a mansion in the desolate cedar and oak atop a switchback of limestone. It had every convenience: swimming pools, tennis courts, stables, golf course, secluded cabins away from the main mansion, a world-class chef, seafood flown in fresh from Maine, women, everything.

"Including a sophisticated alarm system, I'm sure," I added.

"Yeah," J.D. said, smiling, "but nothing an old Indian can't get through."

He must have seen the doubt in my face. He got serious.

"Really, I know how to get in. It's just that after we do what we need to do, I'm not sure how or if we can get out."

"We? You want me to go storming into some mob fortress out in the middle of nowhere with you? That's not exactly what I had in mind. I thought we were going to try to piece together the article Jake was working on and get it published."

"We don't have to piece it together, Ira. Jake had it on a computer disk. If you don't have it, they must. We need to go in there, get the disk, and if we happen to find the bastard that shot Jake, I'm for givin' him a one-way, all-expense-paid trip to hell."

"J.D., I don't think I can do it. This shit is beyond my capabilities. Hell, I'm a schoolteacher."

"Now you are. But you were one hell of a bullfighter a few years back. And you weren't afraid of anything. I've seen you fight bulls with a concussion, broken ribs, and a fractured jaw. You don't quit. Besides, it was my understanding from Jake that the reason you quit the magazine and went to teaching was to have your summers free to start clowning again. In fact, weren't you supposed to be working a show in South Texas this coming weekend?" He looked at me with a slight grin on his face as if to say he knew me better than I did.

I sighed and sank back in my chair. "Okay. You've got me. What are we gonna do?"

"Andy has put on a big rodeo in Llano every year just after Memorial Day for the past twenty or thirty years. That show is next week. Can you get out of your contract for that other rodeo?"

"Sure, the contractor's an old friend. You remember him—Smilin' John Boyd. I'll tell him something has come up. There's a kid who usually works with me who can do the show. He's got a friend that's been hanging around for months, wanting a chance to fight bulls."

"Good. I'll get you the job at Llano and we'll be in."

"But they've already hired the clowns for Llano. I was at the magazine office when the news release came through."

"Yes, but the clown they hired is Ronnie Kramer. Now, if Mrs. Kramer knew about where Ronnie went during some of those 'committee meetings,' Ronnie might not be real welcome back home. I'll give the poop to a friend of mine who will call Ronnie and *suggest* that Llano needs a different clown this year. Before that, though, you can call Ronnie and tell him you've got a show you can't make and were wondering if he'd be willing to do it for you if he's free that weekend. Then, after he gets the call canceling Llano, he'll probably be in touch with you. If not, he doesn't need the money as bad as he always lets on."

"Okay, but if I let the bullfighter that's helping me go on to South Texas, I won't have a partner for Llano to help with acts and the bullfighting."

"You do now, pard. Johnny Deerslayer, clown and bullfighter, at your service."

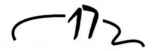

Apparently, J.D. had been doing a little bullfighting at some of the all-Indian rodeos in New Mexico and Arizona. He didn't have to worry about anyone recognizing him. Besides, he said, the Indians sure weren't about to turn him in to the mob.

"It's about rodeo, Ira," J.D. said as we sat in his living room drinking coffee after packing our stuff for the trip. "Indians out here don't have a lot, you know. Just their land and their families. That's the two most important things to them, though. And they can enjoy both of them at their rodeos. They don't leave the land, and they take the whole family along.

"An Indian rodeo ain't like other rodeos. Oh, the sport's the same, but the whole attitude is different. They love this sport, on their terms. An Indian is tied to the land and his family. Won't leave either one, if it's up to him. So here they just put on their own form of rodeo. The contestants don't blow into town for the performance, ride a bronc or bull, then head off for another show just to make money. They stay for the whole shebang. Visit with friends and distant relatives, catch up on news from the far side of the rez or a different rez. It's a lot like the pow-wows and dance competitions. They do it at their own pace."

J.D. turned in his seat to get a better view of me while he continued urgently, like it was something he had to make me understand. I drank some more of Linda's coffee.

"I guess it's kind of like the old ways, you know. They travel around their land, prove their skill and bravery, bring home the spoils of victory, then celebrate. The prize money almost ain't as important as the buckle. And that ain't as important as the prestige they gain within their families, their tribes, and even from Indians from other tribes.

"Anyway," he said, settling back in his seat, "Indians respect a top rodeo hand. Even if I didn't have a drop of Indian blood, I doubt anyone would ever say anything about me, even if they knew the mob was looking for me."

"How come you never see any of these guys in the big rodeos, J.D.? Some of the ones I've seen are good enough."

J.D. snorted. "It's the land and family thing, man. Some of the guys go off and beat the pants off the big boys. Right now, we got some good team ropers and saddle bronc riders. A couple of guys are pretty good bareback riders. We even had one fellow win the bull riding at the world finals a few years back. You should know him. You were clowning it."

"You mean Romero?"

J.D. laughed. "That's him. The girls all call him Romeo. He's one of the best. He could win the IPRA or the PRCA world championship, if he set his mind to it. But he won't. He'd have to travel too much to do that. So he settled for the world finals. All he had to do for that was go to one of their qualifiers, place high enough to make the finals, then outride everyone there. He did. Then he went home, got married, had some kids. He's got a three-year-old who's already winning the mutton bustings at the Indian rodeos."

J.D. looked wistfully out the window at his two boys, climbing all over my truck. "I like these people, Carter. I never knew them much until my *untimely* death," he said, his sense of humor taking over for a second before he became sober again. Then he looked back at me, as serious as I've ever seen him before.

"I ain't missed the outside world one little bit. As soon as this is over, I'm coming back to live out the rest of my days here among my wife's people. I'll try to help them as much as I can with the one thing I really value from the white man's world."

"What's that, J.D.?"

He shrugged and looked past me at the wall. I turned and looked. There, framed on the wall, was a 1956 National Finals Rodeo number. I turned back to J.D., and he smiled a little lopsided grin.

"Hell, *rodeo,* of course! What the hell else would I miss?"

18

J.D. got us in at Llano. The rodeo committee chairman was a middle-aged, pot-bellied, graying man who seemed grateful for us when we pulled up to the contestants' gate.

"I don't know what happened to Kramer, but we were sure lucky you guys were available on such short notice."

I looked at J.D., who was sitting there as innocent as could be, and then told the chairman it had worked out well for us, too.

"I had a committee cancel on me at the last minute, too, so we were free when we got your call."

He pointed toward the back of the chutes, and we thanked him. I backed the clowning trailer with all my acts in it up close to the let-out gate of the arena, where all my stuff would be handy. J.D. got out and stretched. We had driven from Espanola to Hillsboro a week before. J.D. and I had spent a week planning our moves at the hideaway. He'd finally told me that Andy and Frankie always held a big party after the final night of the rodeo for the contestants, clowns, committeemen, stock contractor, and a whole slew of "girls" from Austin and Dallas. They'd party the whole night. If there was ever a time we'd have a chance of finding the guys who killed Jake, that party would be it.

Meanwhile, we had three nights of bullfighting to survive.

We rolled the clowning barrel out of the trailer and pulled out the various suitcases, bags, and boxes that held our gear. As the bullfighter, J.D. had only one suitcase with his pads, cleats, and makeup, plus three freshly laundered pairs of "baggies," oversized Wranglers that had been cut down to miniskirt length, had the seams ripped open, and had been put back together with Velcro so the whole thing would tear away if a bull got a horn hooked inside the baggie waistline or up the leg. J.D. and I had both been at the rodeo in Oklahoma where a bullfighter had nearly died due to the famous strength of his Wrangler baggies. After that, we and almost every other clown and bullfighter had taken to either Velcroing the seams of their baggies or else sewing them back together very lightly with thin thread that would rip in an emergency. Since that night in Oklahoma, the tactic had saved several clowns from serious injury or death.

On the other hand, as the rodeo clown and contract acts provider, I had every nook and cranny of the trailer filled with all sorts of necessities. One box off to the left held all my wigs. In my acts, I changed wigs every time I went into the barrel, to the delight of the crowd. I might go in with a red-and-black punk rock wig, then send it flying out into the arena before popping up moments later with a blue shag or bright yellow Afro wig. Because of that, I had nearly thirty different wigs in the box.

There were boxes of costumes for different acts. I usually did three or four contract acts per night. With a three-night run, that could call for ten or twelve different acts. Usually, though, a committee asked for particular ones, either in advance or after seeing them the first night. Sometimes I would change acts the second night if one didn't seem to be going over well with the crowd. So I set out the three different costumes I would use in the Thursday night performance. We called them "perfs" for short, and tonight's perf would see the Exploding Birthday Cake Act (chef's outfit), the Whodini Disappearing Assistant Act (wizard hat and outfit for me, small version of J.D.'s outfit for the volunteer kid who would help), and the Exploding Baseball Bat Act (a baseball uniform for me and a ball cap for J.D.).

Once those were all set out, I pulled out the "Bomb Case," an old suitcase that held black powder, talcum powder, premade wiring harnesses with switches, extra wire, extra switches, flashbulbs for detonators, cotton balls for wadding, plastic bags and empty toilet paper roles for bomb casings, and black electrician's tape for wrapping the bombs. I quickly made the big bomb for the exploding "gas" stove in the birthday cake act and the three smaller ones for the Whodini magic act. Then I had to load the "clown gun," a black powder cap-and-ball replica of an 1851 Navy Colt that J.D. would shoot at me with when he "reappeared" at the end of the magic act.

I measured off the black powder into each chamber in the revolver's cylinder, then used white toilet paper as wadding. I always made sure the powder came right to the end of the cylinder for two reasons. First, it made a bigger bang. Stock contractors and committees loved a big bang and lots of smoke. Sometimes it doesn't matter what the act is—the bigger the bomb and the more smoke, the bigger laugh it gets. Second, the white toilet paper being visible in the end of the cylinder let me know for sure that the gun was loaded with blanks. No white toilet paper visible, no firing. It was a safety check that I went over with other clowns I worked with. I even left a sticky note stuck to and rubber banded to the handle so they couldn't forget. No white toilet paper, don't fire the gun. Better a messed-up act than a tragic death.

J.D. finished checking the wiring on the exploding stove and sat down on the other end of the tailgate, the black powder, caps, and toilet paper spread between us. He opened the ice chest and grabbed us each a Gatorade. He sat mine down on the tailgate beside me as I poured black powder into the last of the chambers of the cylinder.

I hadn't mentioned much about his disappearance, so I thought now might be a good time. Most everyone had headed somewhere for supper.

"How'd you do it, Johnny?" I asked as I finished up loading the pistol. I'd taken to calling him Johnny Deerslayer during the week before we got to Llano. I didn't want to slip up inside some mob fortress.

"What's that?"

"The death. How'd you do it?"

"It was easy. I'd taken blood samples from cows before, so I just began taking a pint of my own blood every month or so. I stored it in a locked refrigerator in the barn on my place, the one where we kept the cow and horse medicine for the ranch. I was the only one with a key to it. No one ever knew.

"The night of my 'death,' I went to the ranch, got all the blood, drove the truck to the lake, and set up the death scene. I made sure to use enough blood that they wouldn't wonder whether I had survived.

"The worst part, though," he added, picking up the roll of toilet paper and examining it in minute detail, "was putting Linda and the boys through the trauma of thinking I was dead."

He looked from me toward the northwest, just to the right of the setting sun, looking toward where Linda was probably tucking the two boys into bed somewhere a thousand miles away. When he looked back at me, his face was heavy, his eyes sad.

"I'll never be able to make that up to them."

19

I was worried about running into Andy and Frankie until J.D. explained that, while Andy tried hard every year to get down to the rodeo for all three nights, he'd only seen the old man make it two or three years. Usually he was tied up with business up north and didn't arrive until the Saturday night performance.

Frankie, J.D. said, liked to make a dramatic entrance at the very last second. He was scheduled to ride on Saturday night, the final performance. With that information, I was able to breathe a little more freely, and I turned back to showing J.D. how to make the smoke-and-noise bombs I used in my act.

Each bomb started with a toilet paper tube. I had asked the janitor at the college to save the tubes as he replaced them in the school's restrooms. He'd been a little suspicious of me the first time I asked, but one Saturday he came by the house and I showed him how I made the bombs. From then on, he kept me in a steady supply.

I inserted whatever length of telephone wire I needed for the bomb: about three feet for the ones that just went from the front pocket of my baggies back to my butt, where the bomb was hidden by a bandanna, and ten feet for the one that I drug behind me and blew up when I spit "tequila" on the ground.

On the end that I passed through the toilet paper tube, I wired a photo flashbulb. That would serve as the spark to set off the black powder. Then I pulled the bulb down into the paper roll and taped the end to the wire that hung out. That left me with one open end of the tube and one closed end with a flashbulb sitting in that end. I measured out the appropriate amount of black powder for the amount of bang that I wanted. About half full was a pretty big blast, and I reserved ones of that size for bombs that would detonate at least five feet away from anyone. I usually filled the ones on my rear end only about a quarter full. More than that, and even the heavy rubber pad inside my baggies didn't quite shield me from the blast.

The rest of the tube was filled with talcum powder to produce even more smoke than the black powder. In confined spaces, such smoke would take an hour to clear out, but out in the middle of a rodeo arena, it made just the right amount of smoke. Outside, night breezes and no ceiling allowed the smoke to dissipate in a matter of minutes, usually in only seconds.

Once the tube was filled, I began to wrap it with black electrician's tape. The black tape kept the powder dry, but it also determined the power of the explosion. The tighter I wrapped it, the more powerful explosion the compressed powder made. Wrapped looser, there was less bang but still a lot of smoke for the crowd. The wrapping was the secret. I'd seen clowns wrap bombs too tightly and nearly blow a hand off. And I'd seen guys so scared of the bombs that they'd hardly wrapped them at all. That resulted in an embarrassing *"Pffft!"* when it was detonated.

The other end of the wire was connected to a plastic box I'd made from Radio Shack parts and pieces. Inside, a battery connector joined a 9-volt transistor radio battery to two switches. One switch was the actual detonating switch. It was a standard push-button type switch and was the one that I pressed when it was time for the bomb to explode. The other was a sliding-type safety switch that kept the trigger switch from accidentally being pushed until I was ready. I'd learned the hard way that such bombs needed that second switch. The switch box had only a couple of inches of wires hanging out of it. These were connected to the telephone wire that led to the bomb.

I tested each battery and each wire before putting them together. To test the battery, I would place the two leads on my outstretched tongue. The jolt of electricity from joining the two terminals tasted funny and metallic but wasn't harmful. Then I'd hook the switch up to the battery and test its wires. Finally, I'd hook the telephone wire that would eventually lead to the bomb and put those two wires to my tongue while I pressed the trigger switch. The metallic jolt would let me know that the current was going from battery, through switch, and to the wires that would end up connected to the flashbulb. I managed to keep from showing any reaction when I tested the batteries, and I finished my demonstration of the bomb-making process by handing a battery to J.D.

"Test it," I said, as innocently as I could manage, and reached back into the bomb case for another roll of telephone wire. "Just stick your tongue on the terminals and you'll feel the tingle if it's got a charge."

He looked uneasily at me out of the corner of his eyes. "Won't hurt?"

"Naw, it's just a tingle."

He stuck his tongue out and placed the terminals right in the middle. "YOW!" He dropped the battery, jerked his tongue back into his mouth, and spat two or three times, glaring at me. "That hurt," he whined.

I gave him my best doubtful look, picked up the battery from the tailgate, and stuck it on my own tongue without so much as a flinch.

"Aww, come on, J.D.," I said, handing it back to him. "You could hardly feel that. Give me a break and test all these switches, too, would you?" With that, I handed him a bag full of switches I'd built over the winter—eight of them. "And these batteries." I handed him eight fresh batteries, still in their wrapping.

"They're fresh," he said, pointing at the wrappers. "Still in the bag."

"Yeah, but sometimes they've been sitting on the shelf too long. Have to test each and every one of them."

Without looking at him, I got up and went to the front of the truck to sort out my costumes for the night. From the tailgate, I could hear the occasional "Yip!" and spitting that accompanied another battery or switch test. I grinned to myself. It might not even us up for him letting us all think he'd been dead the last few years, but it was a start.

20

J.D. and I brought up the rear of the grand entry at the start of the rodeo, him on a multi-colored mini-bike that put his knees up in his face, me on a skateboard with oversized wheels that he pulled behind the bike on a rope. I goofed around behind the bike like a water skier until we were almost back to the let-out gate. Then I "accidentally" fell off the skateboard, but grabbed it as I went down. Holding on with one hand and waving the other and screaming, I let J.D. haul me out of the arena to the sound of wholesale laughter from the stands.

We pulled up next to the trailer, and I got up and dusted the arena dirt from my baggies. J.D. stowed the bike and skateboard while I grabbed my "bomb pants."

The baggies that I wore were different from the ones J.D. had on. While J.D.'s ended about mid-thigh, having been cut off to accommodate the bullfighting work he would be doing, mine were full-size 54-inch Wranglers that went all the way to my ankles. J.D.'s had the inseam cut out so that they resembled an ugly, huge, denim miniskirt. Mine still had both legs intact. My bomb pants were made of an identical pair of Wranglers with a couple of alterations. First, there was a hole in the left front pocket that allowed me to run a wire to the middle seam just below the belt loops in back. There, another hole allowed the wire to protrude through the baggies just where my butt would be when I bent over. Inside the front pocket, I had hooked that wire to one of the switches J.D. had tested earlier. The other end, on the back seam, was attached to one of the bombs we had made. This one wasn't as powerful as the ones that exploded somewhere other than on my body. Nevertheless, I had a piece of truck flap rubber sewed into a pocket inside the jeans where the bomb rested, and it would take most of the force out of the explosion. I had been extremely grateful for the extra protection the time I accidentally switched the bigger exploding stove bomb with my regular "butt bomb." I still kept the old baggies with the blackened hole in them around to show new clowns or untried bullfighters some of the very real dangers of grown men playing with gunpowder and sparks.

I did the final rigging of the switch inside the front left pocket, twisting the wires together and insulating them with electrician's tape. I did the same thing with the bomb, except that this was not a butt bomb. This one had about a ten-foot wire, wrapped in electrician's tape so that it wouldn't show against the dark arena floor. A length of thin cord was wrapped in so that I couldn't accidentally pull the wires loose. I coiled up the wire, stuffed it and the bomb in the right rear pocket of my pants, grabbed the tequila bottle full of water and food coloring, and headed for the gate.

One of the functions of the rodeo clown, especially the one who brings comedy acts to the rodeo, is to be prepared at all times to fill in when a chute-fighting horse or bull slows down the action in the arena or when some behind-the-scenes emergency causes problems. He is expected to step in with some jokes or a short act, what circus clowns used to call "walk-ons," so that the crowd never suspects anything is out of the ordinary. In order to be prepared for just such happenings, I hung around the let-out gate during the bareback riding event, harassing the gateman, always close to the announcer so that he could whisper to me if he needed me to take up some time. In between each ride, I would stand behind the gateman and mimic his moves.

Carl Gatlin was the gateman that night. I'd worked with him before. He kept trying to trip me up, one of the favorite pastimes of many a rodeo cowboy. The clown was always getting the best of the cowboys, announcers, stock contractors, and others involved in the sport. Rarely did one of them get a chance to embarrass or stump the clown, whose business it was to create a sense of havoc in the arena.

I snuck up behind Carl as he watched the pickupmen bring the first bareback bronc toward the let-out gate after having thrown his rider. Carl never even saw me. I stayed a step or two behind him as he closed the gate and fastened the latch again. Just as he turned around, I hollered, "Boo!" Carl must have jumped a foot high and two back.

At the same time, I exaggerated the same move, grabbed my hat with both hands, screamed, and overemphasized a jump backward, raising both knees as high as possible in the process.

"Ira," came announcer Ray Albert's voice over the sound system, "just what the heck is goin' on down there?"

I fell to my knees and stuck my right hand inside my baggy shirt, then moved it out from my chest as far as it would go and back quickly and repeatedly, representing a fast-beating heart.

"He scared me!" I hollered up at Ray.

"Well, you shouldn't have been following him so close," he said.

"Yeah, well he shouldn't still be wearing his Halloween mask."

Ray pretended to look at Carl. "Ira, that ain't no Halloween mask. It's his regular face."

"Ahhhhhhh!" I screamed, jumping up and running to the opposite side of the arena.

"What's the matter now?"

I stood, knees shaking, pointing a finger at Carl. "Now I'm really scared."

As the crowd chuckled, Ray made sympathetic clucking sounds and then turned back to the next rider. I had to fill in with two or three more jokes before the last horse bucked. Then it came time to switch to the other end of the arena for the calf-roping event.

Because moving from a bucking event to a timed event takes a few minutes—pickupmen leaving the arena, ropers coming in, workers running from the bucking chutes to the roping chutes—I needed to take up two or three minutes.

"Hey, Ray," I hollered up at the announcer as I sauntered cockily into the middle of the arena.

"Yeah, Ira. What's going on now?"

"You hear about my new job?"

"New job? I didn't know you even had a job."

I, of course, looked insulted. "You think this is all I do? I'll have you know I got me one of them university educations. I'm a pre-owned scientist."

"You mean renowned?" Ray asked.

"Yeah, that's what I said. I'm pre-owned, famous all over the world."

"Now, Ira, who in his right mind would give you a job as a scientist?"

Sticking my thumbs in the suspenders of my baggies, I tried to look as proud as I could, jutting my chest out a foot and rocking backward and forward on my feet. With a smug look, I answered him. "Texas A&M University."

"You mean you're an Aggie scientist?"

"One of the best."

"That don't say much for the rest of 'em."

I looked taken aback. "I'll have you know, Ray, that I have invented an amazing new commercial product that will revolutionize and further the close international workings of Mexico and Texas for many years to come."

Behind the microphone, Ray was nodding to the secretary and timers as they showed him the list of contestants for the next event and handed him some index cards of sponsors or queens or some such that had not been announced in the grand entry. He calmly filed them in the fingers of the hand holding the mike and in return handed the secretary the prepared tape he had chosen as the music for the calf-roping. The secretary popped the bareback riding music cassette out of the tape player, handed it back to Ray, and popped the calf-roping tape in. The whole time, he never lost track of our little play-acting conversation. Without missing a beat in the timing, his voice came back to me.

"Now, what in the world could you have invented that would do that?"

I held up the "tequila" bottle, which sloshed nearly full with bright green liquid. "I have combined products from Mexico and Texas to produce a new alcoholic beverage."

Ray conducted a few more administrative details while responding.

"And just what is that?"

"I mixed the Texas jalapeño pepper and the Mexican tequila together."

"And what'd you come up with?"

"Jalapeño tequila," I said proudly, waving the green-juice-filled bottle high over my head.

"I don't believe it."

"Here, let me show you. For the first time, I will tonight taste this never-before-sampled new liquor."

"Now, wait, I wouldn't . . ." Ray stammered.

I pulled the cork, swallowed some of the green water, and immediately bugged my eyes out. I went through some contortions, held my mouth with both hands, danced around in a little circle, and then waved my hands around in the air, pointing at myself with my pointer finger.

"Good gosh, man, that stuff could be killing you. Quick, spit it out!"

With an exaggerated nodding of my head, I arched my back and turned back the way I had come. My dancing had not been as random as it appeared. Along the way, I'd slipped the bomb and wire out of my pocket and dropped it to the ground. Then, I'd stepped away from it to the end of the wire. Now, as I arched my back to spit, I turned to where the bomb lay only ten feet away on the arena floor. I double checked to make sure it wasn't close to anyone, then made an intense exaggeration of spitting in that direction.

I let fly with the spit, flicked the safety off the bomb switch, and depressed the push button trigger all at the same time. Ten feet away, the ground exploded in a shower of bright orange flame and huge billows of white smoke, exactly where I'd aimed my spit. I flipped backward, looking like the explosion had knocked me over. The gasp from the crowd told me that the timing had been perfect. Either that or they had never seen the act before and had been surprised by the explosion.

"Carter," Ray hollered in mock alarm over the sound system, "are you all right?"

I picked myself up and pretended to check all my body parts. "Yeah," I said, "I'm okay."

"Well, I must say that I've never seen anything like that before."

I picked up the tequila bottle, looked at it, then up at Ray. "Yeah, that's got some kick to it, don't it?"

I raised the bottle to my lips, but his voice cut me short.

"No . . . Don't you do that again."

I looked up at him as if perplexed.

"I just got a call. The bomb squad is on its way out right now. I'd get out of here if I was you."

I looked startled and started to run out of the arena, looking for a place to throw the tequila bottle.

"Don't you even think about throwing that bottle in here. You take it out that back gate and throw it in the river."

I ran quickly from the arena gate on the side toward the Llano River. No sooner did I disappear from sight than another explosion and a column of smoke came from out in the parking lot.

"I guess he didn't make it," Ray said. "Ladies and gentlemen, how about a hand for your rodeo clown, Ira Carter."

21

J.D. came walking out of the shadows around the edge of the parking lot, carrying the switch, coil of wire, and what was left of the bomb, still smoking.

"How was that?"

I nodded. "Good timing. Might wait just a second or two next time. Makes it a little more realistic."

He dumped the wiring into the back of the truck and got us each a bottle of Gatorade from the cooler before meeting me at the back of the trailer. I always kept the trailer locked while an act was going on, especially at a show like this one where the crowd could actually get back behind the chutes without too much trouble. I kept the key on an elastic strap around my left wrist. I fished it out and opened the trailer.

The next act was laid out at the edge of the trailer, but we had several minutes to kill before the roping event was over. I shucked the bomb pants long enough to position a butt bomb under the red bandanna that hung from the middle rear belt loop after checking to make sure the spark was still making it through the wire. The Gatorade

and the electricity made some kind of ugly reaction, re-
sulting in a nasty taste on my tongue. I made a face, and
J.D. laughed. I held the end of the wires toward him.

"Want a taste?"

"Oh, no!" he said, backing away quickly, both hands
above his head.

I wired the butt bomb and slipped back into the bomb
pants. The bomb had already been placed in the exploding stove, but I checked it just to make sure it was hooked
up right. A mental checklist confirmed that I had all the
props for the act just as a healthy, well-groomed rodeo
queen type walked up to J.D.

"I'm here," she announced cheerily, the orange lamé-
and-sequined, skin-tight western outfit bouncing merrily
to a stop. I had to give J.D. credit; he could really pick the
girls for the act.

I explained to her that she would have to reapply her
makeup after the act and that she could use our makeup
mirror if she wished, then made sure J.D. had explained
the act to her. He had, and she appeared undaunted.

I quickly covered a round, foam pillow blank with
shaving cream to form a "birthday cake," then added a few
swipes of colored cake icing. It didn't say anything, but
from the stands it would look just like a decorated cake.
The cake slid into a shallow tray inside the stove, and we
were ready for the second act.

As the last roper loped out of the arena, I ran into the
arena from the let-out gate.

"Ray, Ray, Ray!" I hollered, turning every way but toward the announcer's stand.

"What in the world is the matter, Ira?" he answered.

I turned toward him. "Oh, there you are," I said, feign-
ing complete surprise that he should be right where he
had been all night. Behind me, J.D. and another cowboy
we'd recruited were carrying the exploding stove into the
middle of the arena.

George Wilhite 79

"Hey, wait a minute, Ira, you can't bring that in here. We got a rodeo to run. Broncs are gonna be bucking out there in a minute. Get that outta here."

"Hold on, Ray. I got a problem. I met this beautiful girl today and it's her birthday. I promised her I'd make her a birthday cake and I don't know how to cook."

"Not my problem, Ira."

"But I know you're a good cook, Ray. You can help me."

"Nope, got a rodeo to run here. Can't help ya."

I got real quiet and cocked my head to one side. "Ray, your wife know where you was last night?"

Ray took an all-too-audible gulp, all part of the act, and said, "Well, you know, Ira. I could maybe help ya a little."

As J.D. set all the ingredients on top of the stove, I asked, "What do I do first, Ray?"

"You got any eggs?"

"Yep," I said, pulling two big eggs out of a carton.

"Okay, break those into a mixing bowl."

I made a big show of breaking the two eggs and letting the clear liquid and the yolks drop the two feet from my outstretched arms to the mixing bowl on the stove. That done, I deftly dropped the eggshells themselves into the mixing bowl.

"Now put some milk in with the eggs."

I grabbed the old-glass milk bottle that was filled with white colored water, turned quickly and spilled half of it almost on J.D. He took a half-hearted swipe at me as I turned back around and poured the "milk" into the mixing bowl, being absolutely sure to slosh most of it over the side and all over the stove and ground.

"Now beat the eggs."

I stopped, looking confused.

"What?"

"Beat the eggs. Beat the eggs."

"You sure?"

"Look, I said beat the eggs, didn't I? Beat the eggs."

I pulled off my belt and commenced to beat the mixing bowl with it.

"NO! NO! NO!" Ray said. "Not like that. Whip them instead."

"Whip 'em?"

"Yes, whip them, don't beat them."

I reached behind the stove and took the buggy whip I had stashed there. Stepping back, I proceeded to tear into the mixing bowl again, milk-and-egg mixture flying everywhere, even on me.

"That's better," Ray said.

That done, I acted like I was going to put the mix into the stove.

"Wait a minute, Ira," Ray hollered, "you can't put that in yet. You need flour."

"Oops, I almost forgot." I pulled a bag of flour off the top of the stove and began to pour it into the mixing bowl, waving the bag around until a nice thick fog of flour smoke almost obscured the entire act. I kept one corner of the bag pinched, holding just a teaspoon or so of flour in reserve. Then I stopped, like I had just thought of something. "Hey, Ray. How much flour?"

Ray acted as if he were consulting a cookbook in the announcer's stand. "Two cups."

"Okay."

By now I had emptied a five-pound bag of flour all over the stove, the arena floor, and me. The mix obviously had way too much flour in it. Nonetheless, I hunched over the mixing bowl like I was studying it intensely. Then I held my hand out, palm cupped up, and poured the tiniest bit of reserve flour into my hand, dumped it in, studied it once more, and repeated the process. Done, I threw the flour bag over my shoulder and wiped my hands in satisfaction.

"That all?" I asked, turning to the announcer.

"That's it, Ira," he said. "Now put it in the oven and bake it for thirty minutes at 450 degrees."

I put the mixing bowl in the oven, then stood up as if remembering something. "Hey, Ray. How do you turn this thing on?"

Ray feigned exasperation. "You mean you don't already have the oven preheated?"

I raised my shoulders and held both hands out, palm side up, to indicate how stupid I was.

"Is it gas or electric?"

I looked at the back. "Gas."

"Well, turn the gas on and stick a lit match inside the oven to light the pilot."

I turned the big fake red handle marked "GAS" on the back of the stove, then began to pat myself all over, looking for a match. Meanwhile, pink smoke from a bomb I'd lit while turning the "gas" on was beginning to flow out of the stove in all directions.

"Uh, Ira . . ."

"I got a match here someplace, Ray. Just a minute."

"Ira . . ."

"I got it, Ray, I got it," I said, finally pulling a match out of one pocket, then turning to stick my head into the open stove amid the pink smoke.

"Ira . . . I wouldn't . . ."

While Ray was setting it up, I struck the match on the outside of the stove where the crowd could see it flare up, then brought it inside the stove with me. Only my butt was sticking out of the wooden box. I dropped the match, grabbed the bomb switch on the floor of the stove and the butt bomb switch in my pants pocket, flipped the safeties off, and pressed both triggers at the same time.

In this act the butt bomb is really just a backup in case the bomb on top of the stove, set safely into a stout metal cup that pointed to the sky, didn't go off. But along the way I'd found that firing both bombs at the same time produced an even better effect than just the top of the stove exploding. Timed right, both bombs went off simultaneously, creating the illusion that the top of the stove exploded and the blast found its way right out my butt.

I jumped back out of the stove and the smoke, the bandanna on my butt on fire. As I dropped my butt to the ground and scooted on it across the arena floor, hollering as loud as I could, the crowd couldn't hear me over their own laughter.

"Good gosh, Ira. You've done gone and done it now. That cake is blown to smithereens."

I got up, shook my head, and reached back into the stove to retrieve the foam-and-shaving-cream cake from its tray. I held it overhead and pointed toward the let-out gate.

"Here she comes, Ray, here she comes."

I started running toward Miss Orange Rodeo as if delighted to see her. People in the crowd started murmuring and laughing. Many of them knew the local rodeo sweetheart and wondered what her part was in all this.

As I got within five feet of her, I whispered, "Here it comes," and pretended to trip.

I could see her close her eyes, then the cake hit her full in the face. For a moment, the crowd was totally silent, not knowing whether this was part of the act or not. Then the rodeo queen turned on her heel, stuck her nose up in the air, and walked out of the arena, apparently highly disgruntled with her new beau. I followed on my knees, hands clasped prayer-like in front of me, apparently begging forgiveness right out the let-out gate.

Within seconds, the crowd was in an uproar, having decided it was okay to laugh.

Outside the gate, J.D. had sent two cowboys in to retrieve the stove and table while he helped the queen get the shaving cream off her face. He was handing her paper towels and baby wipes in succession. As the cream came off her face, we could see her smile spreading from cheek to cheek.

"That was fun," she chirped happily as three other rodeo sweethearts rushed to her side, laughing and carrying on. "Can I do it again tomorrow night?"

22

After cleaning up the mess from that act, we managed to get through the bronc riding and team roping without needing a walk-on.

This was the worst time of the whole rodeo—between acts. During the acts, I was busy and had to force myself to concentrate on what I was doing. That part was easy. For the past seventeen years, whether riding or clowning, I'd learned how to "put my game face on" and tune out the outside world while I took care of business. But between acts, all I could think about was our upcoming mission. Whether or not we'd be able to get the disk back. Whether or not we'd get caught by Andy, whom we both considered an old friend. Whether or not Andy knew about what had happened. Hell, whether we'd be alive next week. In the back of my mind, I was wondering if the disk even existed anymore. Why would they keep it?

J.D. brought me back to reality with a tap on the shoulder. "You okay?"

I shrugged. "Yeah ... uh ... sure. Just double-checking that this was ready," I said, holding up the magic wand I'd use in the next act.

J.D. tilted his head and looked at me. "Right. It's a wooden dowel with red and gold ribbon wrapped around it. Pretty complex, all right," he said, then slapped me on the shoulder and grinned. "Well, the roping's over, so gather up your little fairy wand and let's go."

As the last team roper left the arena, J.D. and I waltzed into the arena with my Whodini act to fill time while the workers started setting up barrels for the barrel race. Now, barrel racers are known to be picky, and we could tell that setting barrels tonight was going to take quite a while when three of the barrel racers, each with her own tape measure, walked out behind the workers to check the measurements. But that's why I usually kept the Whodini act until the barrel racing—it was one act I could lengthen or shorten pretty easily while inside the arena, if necessary.

J.D. and one of the steer wrestlers carried the tall red box out in front of the bucking chutes. The box had black and gold shooting stars painted all over it and huge yellow letters proclaiming "Whodini" on each side.

"Ira," Ray moaned in a weary-sounding voice, "are you back again? I thought we'd seen the last of you tonight."

I shook my head, pulled a wadded-up sorcerer's hat out of the folds of my huge pants, and donned it, the tip falling perfectly in front of my face and tickling the end of my red-painted nose. I exaggerated the facial and body movements of trying to blow it away from my face a couple of times, then reached up as angrily as I could appear to be and knocked it aside with my hand.

"Nope," I said, standing to attention and looking straight up at Ray. "I got me a new act."

"A new act? What is it THIS time?"

I stuck my chest out as far as I could get it, strutted over to my Whodini booth, and stuck my nose even farther up in the air. "Why, just this afternoon, at a garage sale right here in Llano, I found a wondrous, miraculous, fantastic artifact direct from the pages of magic's history."

Ray pretended to cover a yawn with one hand. "Looks like a big, gross, badly painted wooden box to me."

I acted as if he had slapped me in the face, stumbling back and getting a pained look on my face. "I cannot believe you said that. This is a monument to one of the finest magicians of all time—Harry Houdini!"

Ray snorted. "Ira, Houdini is spelled H-O-U-D-I-N-I."

"Aha," I gloated, "I thought exactly the same thing. But the man that had it for sale explained that to me." I smiled like the Cheshire Cat and walked proudly around in a circle, my thumbs hooked behind my bright red suspenders.

"Oh," Ray said, "and just what is that explanation?"

Looking from side to side, I put my hand up by my mouth as if I were whispering to Ray, fifteen feet above me in the announcer's stand.

"It's the way they spell it here in Llano, kinda like a nickname."

"Oh . . . I see."

"Yep, I got it cheap, too. He hadn't told anybody else about it."

"And exactly what does this here Houdini box do, Ira?"

I stopped, cocked my head to one side, and looked quizzically at Ray for a moment as I walked around the box. "Well, Ray, I don't rightly know. The fellow couldn't remember exactly what it does. He thought it might be a disappearing box."

Out of the corner of my eye, I noticed that the three barrel racers and the guy putting out the barrels had gotten into an intense argument over the placement of the first barrel. Betty Hargrove, a West Texas ranch cowgirl who was currently sitting third in the standings, had the little wiry guy setting the barrels cornered between the first barrel and the Dodge Dually he was using to haul the barrels in. The barrel man was only about five feet, four inches tall and as skinny as a rail. Betty, on the other hand, stood about five feet, nine inches and was, to say the least, "larger than average," weighing somewhere in the neighborhood of 200 pounds. Nobody, even the officials of the Professional Women's Rodeo Association, had ever had enough guts to ask Betty her actual weight. Consequently, that part of the contestant statistics on previous world champs (Betty had won the world twice already in barrel racing) was blank in the media guide produced by the association.

It looked like I probably ought to start stretching the act out, I thought as I resumed my conversation with Ray.

"I thought I'd use Johnny to see how the thing works."

J.D. shook his head vigorously, but I grabbed him by the back of his suspenders, opened the door, and "booted" him inside with my foot. As I closed the door, I could already see the black curtain that hung halfway to the back of the box moving aside as J.D. and the kid he'd recruited started to change places.

J.D. had found the boy hanging around the trailer after the last act, asking lots of questions about our act. He'd sent the kid to find his parents so they could give approval for the youngster to participate in the Whodini act. They'd okayed it, and J.D. had gotten the kid dressed for the act.

First, he gave the boy one of the spare shirts that matched his. The arms dragged the ground and, when the kid lifted his arms, half of the sleeve hung down. Then he was given a spare pair of baggies. While they only went to mid-thigh on J.D., the short pants touched the ground on the nine-year-old. The final outfitting was taking place inside the box now, as J.D. was shoving his pink straw clown hat down on the kid's head. We'd checked the fit to make sure it came down far enough to hide his face. On this kid, it went past his ears and didn't stop until it got below his eyes. There was even enough room for him to see out of the bottom of the hat so he could walk.

I pulled a "magic wand" out of my pants, yelled *"Abracadabra,"* and struck the box three times with the wand. On the third strike, J.D. fired one of the bombs from inside the box and a cloud of smoke appeared in front of the door. As the smoke cleared, the door creaked slowly open. Out of the cloud of smoke, a three-foot-tall figure, clad in clothes ten times too big for him, stumbled into the lights of the arena. The hands shook above his head with the half-empty sleeves flopping around as the boy walked in circles, acting as if he were confused by the sudden change from a five-foot, eleven-inch frame to his present size.

I grabbed my head with both hands and turned every which way.

"O-o-o-o-h, Ray!" I hollered. "Somethin' went wrong. What do I do?"

Ray shook his head with the semblance of a man who had reached the end of his rope.

"I don't know, Ira. I told you that you ought not to do this. But, no, you had to try. Maybe you ought to put him back in there and try again."

I acted like the idea had never occurred to me and nodded quickly. Grabbing the kid by the shoulders, I guided him back to the box, opened the door, and put him inside. Immediately, I grabbed the wand, said the magic word, and knocked three times on the box with the wand.

Again, a cloud of smoke erupted. This time, however, the figure that came out was even smaller. Through the smoke, a foot-high figure walked, this time on four legs.

"Oh, my God, Ray . . ."

Buck, my white English bull terrier, wandered out of the smoke, clad in a tiny shirt just like J.D.'s blue-and-white striped one and tiny little baggies. His white tail wagged happily as he bounced around the arena.

George Wilhite 89

"Ira, you've done it now," Ray said, his voice nearly lost in the whoops and hollers from the crowd. "First, you shrunk Johnny. Now, you've changed him into a dog. I bet that's not even Johnny now."

I gathered the dog up, held it up close to my face, and studied it hard. Then I turned to Ray, held the dog up where he could see it, and shouted, "Yep, that's Johnny."

Ray looked skeptical. "How can you tell?"

I pulled one of the dog's legs out full length to show him. "Look at them white legs!"

Again, the crowd reacted, and I hustled Buck off to the box, shoved him in, and closed the door. I backed away, shaking my head. "I don't know what to do, Ray. How will I ever get Johnny back?"

Ray, too, shook his head. "I don't know, Ira. You miss him already?"

"Hell, no, Ray. But the bull riding is coming up, and *Ira* sure ain't fighting no bulls. That's what I brought Johnny along for."

Ray pondered the situation for a moment before calling down to me. "Ira," he said thoughtfully, "you might try another magic word. Maybe 'Abracadabra' isn't the right word."

I snapped my fingers and ran to the box. "You're right. I bet I need a different word."

I grabbed my wand, raised it, and yelled, *"Alacazam!"* striking the box three times in quick succession.

The bomb went off on the third strike and the door opened slowly outward. Suddenly, J.D. stepped out full-size and on two legs through the smoke. I ran toward him, but Ray called out a warning.

"Ira, look out! He doesn't look any too happy to see you ... And he's got a gun."

I came to a sliding stop, then turned and ran for the let-out gate as J.D. looked all around, apparently trying to find me. I jumped onto the gate, bent over at the waist with my head on the outside and my butt on the inside.

On the way up, I'd found the bomb switch in my pocket and thumbed off the safety switch as soon as I saw that the security guards had kept this part of the gate clear of spectators. As my butt went into the air, I heard the blank in J.D.'s revolver go off. I pressed the trigger button and felt the hard impact of the butt bomb explosion even before I heard the noise or saw the flash and smoke between my legs. I hung half over the let-out gate, head upside down outside the gate and my butt exploding on the inside of the gate. Flopping over the gate as if the explosion had blown me over, I kept one hand on the top rail of the gate to allow me to twist and land feet first and look back into the arena. J.D. was following me out, and the crowd was ecstatic. I heard Ray mention our names as J.D. joined me outside the let-out gate, but I was already on my way to the trailer to get rid of my bomb pants and put on my regular ones for the bull riding.

23

I was changed and had my barrel out of the trailer by the third barrel racer. I sat on the barrel and drank a Gatorade just outside the let-out gate while watching the remaining seven riders. The girls were using the alleyway between the bucking chutes to run in and out of the arena, so I wasn't in their way. It was nice to have a show where I didn't have to dodge wild barrel horses when I really needed to get my mind on the event that followed—bull riding.

Betty Hargrove, the barrel racer who'd been hounding the guy setting barrels, was the last racer to run. She shaved nearly half a second off the time of the best run and set a new arena record, putting her in first place after the opening night round ended.

As Betty's horse, Dusty, went out the alleyway, I followed the Dodge Dually back into the arena. It headed for the first barrel to pick it up, and I rolled my clowning barrel to a spot about midway between the first and third barrels, about a third of the way down the arena. I tipped the red, white, and blue contraption up on its end and climbed up on top.

My barrel most closely resembles a giant beach ball—big, round, and puffed up with air. In fact, the basic barrel is made of heavy-gauge steel. A lot of clowns like aluminum barrels, but I'd seen too many of them tossed head-high across the arena by bulls. One had hit a bullfighter friend of mine square in the face as he came in to get the bull off a downed bull rider. He'd been in a coma for a week. That's why I'd decided to go back to the old steel barrel. It weighed a lot more and made it harder for a bull to get it airborne.

Most clowning barrels look like a huge beer keg. Mine, stripped of all its outer coverings, looks more like a pregnant beer keg about to explode. On the top end—the end the clown goes in and out of—there is a hole. Inside I stored hats and props, even a backpack-type water gun, full of water.

I checked to make sure none of the props or padding had moved when I'd rolled the barrel out. I also checked the outside covering and padding to make sure there weren't any obvious rips or tears. The outside of the metal barrel has a layer of closed cell foam wrapped around it, not only to cushion the clown from the impact, but also to protect the bull's head and horns.

While atop the barrel, I struck a pose like a Greek statue—one leg raised behind me, one arm out in front, the other out behind, my chin stuck up in the air. A couple of kids laughed. Funny how you can hear one or two small laughs, what with the announcer doing his thing, the diesel truck purring around the arena, the barrels clanging into the back of the bed, and the audience talking. But when you're doing something that is supposed to be funny and you're waiting for that first indication that it's working, you hear even the smallest snicker. I heard one of the older kids say, "Goofy clown."

George Wilkite 93

I yelled at Ray to get his attention, then pretended to lose my balance. It took me a good five or six seconds of going one way and then another before I actually "fell" off the barrel. By then, everyone was watching. I did an exaggerated back flip and would have landed on my feet if I hadn't intentionally pulled them up at the last minute. As it was, I landed smack square on my butt with a little assist from my feet and legs to cushion the impact.

Ray commented on my lack of coordination and started into his spiel about how the bull riders in the upcoming event would need all of the coordination they had to stay on top of the wild bulls: ". . . monstrous mounds of muscle . . . snorting, hulking beasts . . . like deadly dragons versus modern-day knights of the West . . . two tons of hell-born fury . . ."

The crowd was loving it. I noticed several kids hanging over the top of the fence in anticipation of their favorite event. It was a dangerous place to be.

"Ray . . ." I said, loud enough for him to hear me, but low enough that the crowd couldn't. Ray's eyes glanced my way, and I motioned with my head toward the kids on the fence. He acknowledged it with a quick look their way and a slight nod of his head.

"Ladies and gentlemen, bull riding has been voted the most dangerous sport in the world by the top American sportswriters—guys who've seen everything sports has to offer. More dangerous than skydiving, more dangerous than race car driving, more dangerous than professional football. And all for good reason.

"These bulls, some weighing a ton or more, can crush a cowboy's skull like an egg. One foot or one horn can injure, maim, or kill in a fraction of a second. Because of that, we ask that all you young buckaroos and buckarettes along the fence hop down and take a safe seat in your mom's or dad's lap. Parents, please keep your children off the fence. A bucking bull doesn't always know where his feet are going. And even when he does know, he doesn't care."

Several moms and a dad or two scrambled down out of the stands to gather up wayward kids, and pretty soon the fence was clear. And just in time. Within seconds of the last youngster dropping off the fence, Ray was announcing the first bull rider.

"Jay Hawkins, a Rocksprings, Texas, cowboy, will start off our bull riding tonight. Jay's drawn Double Deuce, Number 22 in the bull riding string."

While I listened to Ray's commentary, my real attention was focused on Chute 4. Contractors liked to start with the back gate usually so that they could be loading more bulls as the front bulls are bucked. J.D. was standing in front of the chute, looking in. He turned toward me and held up his left hand to make sure I knew this cowboy was a lefty.

Which hand a cowboy rides with is important to the clowns because it lets them know when a cowboy is likely to hang up, depending on which way he bucks off a bull. A left-handed rider who bucks off on the left side of his bull, or "into his hand," is not likely to hang up. That's because the handhold in the bull riding rope has a lot of open space on that side of the hand. However, the other side of the handhold has a riser, a piece of stiff leather that provides some clearance for the cowboy's gloved hand. The cowboy runs his hand right up against the riser before he pulls the rope tight. Lefties have a riser on the right side of the handhold and righties have a riser on the left side of the handhold. So, if a lefty bucks off to the right side of the bull or a righty bucks off to the left side, his chance of hanging up is increased. Because of this, a clown will be watching for indications that a lefty is going to buck off to the right side and vice versa for a righty. As the ride progresses, if the bullfighter sees that the rider is leaning farther and farther "away from his hand," the bullfighter will start working his way to where he needs to be to help the cowboy get off.

I jumped up on the top of my barrel and sat there for a second as a cowboy hopped up on the chute gate to pull Jay's rope. As he pulled it, I swung my legs from outside the barrel and let them drop inside the top opening. As the cowboy dropped off the chute gate and moved away, the gateman got ready to lift the latch at the bull rider's signal. I went ahead and dropped down into my barrel, making sure my feet went wide enough to miss the foot-wide square hole in the barrel's bottom. The square hole allows me to stick my feet out of the bottom of the barrel, grab two rope handles inside the barrel, and lift it off the ground with my feet still on the ground. Then I can maneuver the barrel where I want it. This time I waddled my way to the right a little, knowing that the Deuce had a tendency to spin to the right just outside the gate. That would be throwing the cowboy into his hand. Not much chance of a hangup, but he might need a place to hide when he hit. I dropped the barrel down about thirty feet away from the chute, drew my legs up onto the flat metal floor welded into the bottom of the barrel, and knelt down until just my shoulders and head were above the top opening.

I saw Jay's hat move forward and then saw the brim move up and down several times rapidly, "nodding" his head for the gate to open. Jay was a good little bull rider, but I was pretty sure he was outmatched by the Deuce. The Hill Country cowboy had been riding for only about a year, and this was his first matchup with a bull like the big red brindle.

The gateman lifted the latch, opened the gate about a foot to make sure the bull was looking for the opening, then slung it aside rapidly. Another member of the chute help stood on the opposite side of the gate to catch it as it swung wide. The brindle made a half turn out of the chute, going high and hard. Jay was in perfect shape as the bull came up in the front end—chin down, free arm parallel to the ground, hand palm down and out in front over the bull's right shoulder. As the bull reached the top of his jump and dropped his head and shoulders, Jay moved his hips forward and brought his free arm back to even with his shoulder, still palm down and parallel to the ground. His chin was still welded to his chest, his four-inch black felt hat brim hiding his face from sight. The bull hit the ground hard, swinging his head to the left.

The bull's head and two-foot-long horns swung right under Jay's face. If the young cowboy kept his eyes fixed to his gloved riding hand or just in front of it on the top of the bull's shoulder blades, he'd weather the bull's next move. If he didn't, he was as good as thrown. I saw just the faintest flicker of movement from Jay's hat brim as his eyes followed the bull's head to the left. Old cowboy adage: Where the eyes go, the butt follows. No sooner had the Deuce's head moved left than his feet pushed off the opposite way. The bull was starting his buck to the right with his head still turned to the left. Swinging his head that way enabled the old bull to get added centrifugal force to his spin. As the bull's front legs lifted off the ground, his head went back to the right twice as fast as it had come left. But Jay's eyes were still glued to where the head had been only a micro-second before. With no head there to get in the way, Jay had a perfect bird's-eye view of the arena floor just outside his left knee and the Deuce's left shoulder. Probably in that same micro-second, he knew he'd made a mistake. But it was too late.

He tried to turn his head back to the right and buried his chin into his right shoulder. He tried to move his free arm back to keep himself in the middle, but, like most new bull riders, he overcompensated. The movement took his free arm behind his right shoulder, turning his shoulders into the direction of the spin, but too far. Now his right shoulder was pointed at the bull's rump instead of both his shoulders being square with the bull's front end. As the bull's back feet kicked up, Jay's shoulders were to the outside of the spin, lifting his butt off the bull's back and moving all his weight to the outside and down. Jay got "chili-whopped," his head and shoulders slamming down onto the arena floor. Even though arena floors are disced and harrowed before a performance to make them soft, the constant traffic out of the bucking chutes during a performance packs down the dirt right in front of the chutes. The arena dirt was just about two notches this side of concrete by the time the bull riding had started. Jay never moved once he hit the ground.

J.D., knowing Jay's limited experience and the Deuce's bucking style, had positioned himself to the left of the bucking chute, looking at the chutes from my barrel in the arena. He was right there to get the brindle's attention and would have led him away except the only way he could take him would have been right over Jay's limp body. The bull snorted at J.D. once, his head facing into the open chute and his butt out toward me. But he was already looking away from J.D. and getting ready to come around to the right again in a high-diving spin. That jump would take him right around to Jay again. And the Deuce would hook.

As soon as I'd seen Jay go limp, I'd started out of the barrel. By the time J.D. had his attention, I was two steps toward the fallen cowboy. I made the next four steps in the time it took the brindle to make that next jump. I was there one step ahead of him. That last step carried me over Jay's body and put my right foot on the ground in between the Deuce's two-foot horns and Jay. As the bull's back feet hit the ground from the jump, he dropped his head, gathered my right thigh up on his bony forehead, and flipped his mighty neck muscles up. I had one horn in front of my stomach and the other behind my butt as he lifted that head up. I felt the heavy, hard impact of the bony forehead into the muscle of my thigh, realized that the contact was well below the waist, and waited for that dizzying circle of streaks and disorientation that comes when your feet are taken out from under you in the middle of a jump at top speed. My head pitched sideways to the right. I was waiting for the whipping fall to the ground and the impact of my head . . . or shoulders . . . or hip . . . or whatever.

But it didn't come. Instead, I felt the prickly, short-haired brindle hide that covered the bull's massive neck muscles smack my right shoulder. He'd taken my legs out from under me with his hooking, but instead of flying past his head at an angle and smacking the chutes or the arena dirt, my arc to the dirt had been interrupted by the top of the bull's neck.

Lifting his head to hook me had raised his front feet off the ground and carried them over the top of Jay's body to land on the other side. With my legs dangling in his eyes between the horns, he didn't have to look for anything else to hook. He dropped his head again and lifted it, this time sending my feet up into the air. But with most of the weight of my body on his neck instead of his head, he just flipped my feet up and away without throwing my body. The movement threw my feet over my head and I let them go, making a little half somersault that carried me over his right shoulder and planted my feet into the softer arena dirt out away from the front of the chutes.

The last hooking had carried us about ten feet past Jay's body. As my feet touched the ground, I saw two cowboys pulling Jay back into the chute and the gateman clanging it shut. J.D. had stepped around in the meantime and picked up the brindle's head, leading him away from me out into the arena. He made a couple of close passes to impress the crowd, each one leading the bull farther from me and the now safe Jay. Then he took a sudden turn to the right and let the bull pass. The two pickupmen started herding the bull toward the let-out gate.

I stopped suddenly as the world returned to normal. As usual with a hooking, the announcer was aware of where each of us was. He saw me stamp my foot, and he immediately responded.

"Well, Ira? You okay?"

Again, I stomped my foot and reached up and touched my red-and-black punk rock wig. "Ray, I think he mussed my hair."

"How can you tell?"

I acted upset and shook a finger at him. "Hey, now . . . uh-oh!"

"What now?"

I looked closely at the finger I'd shaken at him. "And I think I broke a nail, too!"

The crowd laughed tentatively, not sure if it was okay after a wreck like that. Ray helped 'em out a little.

"Ladies and gentlemen, that's what your rodeo clowns and bullfighters are out there for, to protect the bull riders. How about a hand for a job well done?"

The crowd applauded loudly, now sure of the response expected from them. About that time, the chute gate opened and Jay stepped out, holding his left shoulder with his right hand and rolling the arm around in big circles, trying to get some feeling back in it. A medic with the Justin Healer program stepped out with him and nodded up at Ray.

"And how about a hand for Jay Hawkins? Jay looks to be all right, but he won't be taking much else home tonight except a sore shoulder and your applause."

The clapping increased as Jay raised his hat to the crowd. On his way out of the arena, he stopped for a second between me and J.D.

"Thanks, guys. I don't remember any of it, but they told me you took a hookin' for me."

He reached out his hand. I shook it.

"No problem, Jay. That's why they pay us these fabulous salaries."

"Yeah, well, it still means a lot to me when someone takes a shot intended for me. Thanks."

He nodded to us both and stepped out of the arena.

"Good kid," J.D. said, turning around to face the next chute. "Thanks for getting there. I couldn't turn the bull without taking him right over the boy."

I reached up and patted J.D. on the shoulder, then tried not to limp too badly on my way back to my barrel.

The rest of Thursday night's bull riding went without a hitch. J.D. had to take two other bulls away from fallen cowboys, but he didn't need my help doing it. They were both routine get-offs. I stayed in the barrel and tried to be funny. My hip wouldn't let me do much else that night.

I'd taken the full brunt of the hooking on my thigh muscles and bone. The more I sat in the barrel, the stiffer I got in that leg. It wasn't broken, but I was sure going to have a bruise on it when I woke up in the morning.

J.D. came over to the barrel with a big grin on his face beneath the painted-on one. "Years gettin' to you?" he joked.

"Ain't the years . . . it's the miles."

"Maybe you ought to settle down, get married, and raise a bunch of rugrats."

I gave him an even more pained face, but inside, the thought didn't sound so bad. When I'd first started rodeoing, like all young hands, I'd thought that marriage was about the same as a death certificate. But lately, the traveling and the loneliness had been getting to me. Add a good hurt or two along the way, and a fellow could get plumb depressed. I guess Jake's death was hitting harder now than before. And being around J.D. and his family made me realize how much family meant and how little family I had. Having someone to come home to sounded pretty good.

J.D. seemed to pick up on my mood and let it slide, helping me roll the barrel out to the trailer in deference to my well-abused thigh. A quick check of it in the cab of the truck revealed an already purple-turning-to-blue bruise that ran from my hip joint almost down to my knee. After five minutes of trying, I decided that a pickup cab wasn't the place to undress, so I pulled the big, loose pants back up, used skin cream to get the grease paint off my face, and stepped back out of the truck just as a pair of headlights swept the cab.

A red Dodge Dually pulled up beside our rig and a blonde-haired, denim-capped head popped out of the driver's window.

"Hey, cowboy, you new in town?"

Even hurting, I had to smile at the line. Chelsey Leskowitz, DVM, sat behind the steering wheel and grinned at me.

"Yeah, just here for the weekend. How about a good time, lady?"

"Sure, soon as I find a stall, get my horse watered, fed and hayed, park the trailer, unhook it, lock the saddle and tack up, and get to my motel room, I'll slip into something slinky and you can take me dancing. Of course, it may be four o'clock by then."

J.D. stepped up and tipped his hat.

"Well, ma'am, I don't think this young coot will be doing any dancing tonight. He took a good hooking earlier tonight. He's walking kinda wimpy right now."

Immediately, Chelsey's joking mood turned to concern. In one fluid, practiced motion, she dropped the diesel into neutral, set the parking brake, and was out the driver's side door. She'd dealt with more than enough emergencies in her life, and was able to get out of a car faster than most people I'd known. She stopped just short of me and looked me over from top to toe.

"Where'd he get you?"

J.D. was delighting in my discomfort. He knew I hated going to doctors, and he was pretty sure I'd be embarrassed with a girl fussing over me. What he didn't know was that Chelsey was a vet. Without waiting for my answer, Chelsey looked at my clowning pants that I still had on and nodded knowingly.

"Leg or butt?"

"Leg," I found myself saying.

"Upper or lower?"

"Upper."

She nodded again. "Muscle or bone?"

"Muscle."

"Well, let's get a look at it," she said, rolling up her sleeves and starting toward me.

"Whoa, now, Chelsey. If I could get out of these pants, I'd have already done it. I'm waiting to get back to the motel so I can get 'em off easier."

She stopped. "Good idea." Then she turned to J.D. "Can you get him to the motel while I unload?"

J.D. shook his head. "No, ma'am, I got a better idea. I'll unload your horse and take care of him. You take Ira to the motel and see if you can fix him up."

She looked at me. She didn't know J.D. and wasn't sure if she should leave her horse with him. On the other hand, she was worried about me. Somewhere deep down inside, a little warm spot tried to let me know how good that felt, having somebody worry over me. I nodded at her and then motioned toward J.D.

"Johnny's okay. He knows his way around horses. I can vouch for him."

I suddenly realized how much Chelsey really did trust me when she turned to J.D. and started explaining what needed to be done. I'd never seen her let anyone else take care of Spider.

"I've got a room at the motel, number 106," she told him. "You can drop the truck and keys off there when you're finished. Maybe I'll know more about your barrel-man by then."

J.D. tipped his hat again, slid into the seat of her truck, and started to put it in gear. Chelsey reached behind the cab, popped the tool box to get a bag, and carried it back to my truck.

"Get in, cowboy. Doctor's orders."

25

After having watched me climb gingerly into the truck, ease out of the truck, and limp to the motel room door, Chelsey already had a good idea of what was wrong.

"Quit it. I ain't a horse," I bellowed at her as I walked very carefully over the doorstep.

"Quit what?"

"Watching me walk from behind like I'm a hurt horse."

I flopped as best I could on the edge of the bed. She closed the door and walked toward me, setting her bag down beside the bed. She reached up toward my pants.

"Shuck 'em, cowboy."

I slipped the suspenders off my shoulders and tried to raise my butt off the bed and push the pants down at the same time, but she stopped me.

"Just put your hands behind you and raise your butt off the bed with your good leg."

I did as I was told, and she slipped the baggy britches down to my knees. She stopped there and reached up for the psychedelic tights I wore underneath. As they peeled away, she saw the bruise. Her lips stretched tight.

"Good job, Ira. You got nailed good. Feel broken?"

I set my butt back down on the bed and let her pull the baggies and the tights off.

"Nope. Feels bruised and sore and, most of all, stiff. Can't hardly move my leg from there down."

She looked at me with that look reserved for people who ask if they are all right after falling off a 100-foot cliff.

"Well, yeah. I guess so. That muscle moves your lower leg. The calf moves your foot. So when the top muscle is out of commission, you have to move the whole leg with your other muscles. Don't go anywhere."

She got up and left, returning in a few minutes with a wastebasket full of ice from the motel ice machine. She helped me get out of the rest of my clothes and into the bathtub. Then she wrapped a towel around my leg and put ice on it.

"That will constrict the blood vessels and slow or stop the flow of blood into the area. You should have done it as soon as it happened. It would have helped more."

Just then, there was a knock at the door. She left me, naked and freezing in the bathtub, to answer it. J.D. handed her her keys when she opened the door.

"How is he?"

She looked over her shoulder toward the bathroom. "He'll live, but I think he needs some professional medical attention. I'd like to keep him overnight for observation."

J.D. grinned and nodded. "Yes, ma'am. I'll be down in 240 if you need me for anything."

I knew these two couldn't have planned this, but they sure seemed intent on putting the squeeze play on me.

26

I woke up about 8:00 in the morning, stiff and sore, to the smell of perfume and coffee. Chelsey was already up and laying out a bunch of stuff from a plastic sporting goods store bag on the dresser.

I felt something warm on my leg and looked down. She had already unwrapped and set up a heating pad on my thigh. At the dresser she was pulling out several gel packs that hunters use to keep warm. She looked up and caught my glance.

"Heating pad will help the blood flow better now. You can use these packs during the day and tonight."

One good thing about a woman who knows rodeo and rodeos herself is that you don't have to explain going to work hurt. She'd run barrels with a broken leg herself. It's just part of the game.

She pulled two steaming cups of coffee out of a bag and handed me one.

"I can go get donuts if you want, but I didn't know if you wanted that or a real breakfast. Wouldn't hurt to feed that body while it heals itself."

"Breakfast sounds nice. There's a little café down the road all the guys go to. We could go there and get some eggs."

She nodded and grabbed my canvas bag to pull out a pair of underwear and a T-shirt.

"You might want to get dressed," she said, throwing the clothes at me.

I noticed for the first time that I was buck naked. It wasn't the first time I'd been that way around Chelsey, but for some reason this time it seemed a little embarrassing.

She laughed. "Blushing? You?" Then her voice softened. "Hey, get those on. If you need any help, holler."

I managed the underwear and shirt without her help and stood up.

"How about handing me a pair of Wranglers out of there? Or you gonna make me walk all that way for the exercise?"

"Nope," she said and reached into the bag again.

Out came a pair of loose khaki shorts and some slip-on surf shoes. She threw them on the bed beside me.

"I think those will be easier to get on than Wranglers and boots, don't you?"

I had to agree with that.

"Besides, that muscle has swelled up, and you probably couldn't get your jeans over it. I checked it last night after you conked out. Your knee is fine. That had me worried. We ought to take you down to the hospital to get some X-rays just to be sure there's not a hairline break or something in that upper leg. But I know you don't like hospitals, so I called a friend of mine, a vet here. He'll take an X-ray of your leg, just for me. I told him I wanted to get it framed."

Five minutes later, we were headed for the café. Chelsey had pulled more stuff out of the bags and had me decked out in a wild, flowered Hawaiian print cap that closely matched the Jimmy Buffet T-shirt she'd thrown me from my bag. With my own shades and the shorts and surf shoes, I looked like an authentic tourist.

Inside the café, we found J.D. in a corner, in more ways than one. He was sitting at a corner table with his back to the wall, listening to a constant barrage of chatter from the youngster we'd saved the night before in the bull riding. He raised his hand and motioned for us to join them but couldn't get a word out.

When the kid saw J.D. motion, he turned and caught sight of us. He stood up and took his hat off, then stepped deftly around one chair and pulled it out for Chelsey. She gave me one of those "some-people-know-how-to-treat-a-lady" looks and sat down. I limped around to the other side of the table and sat down. The kid resumed his place and his talking.

"Sir, ma'am . . . I was just thanking Mr. Deerslayer for last night—"

I held up a hand until the kid saw it and stopped. "Son, didn't anybody ever tell you that Indians like silence? Johnny here is one of those old-time Indians who don't like a lot of noise. Bothers him something fierce."

I pushed the bill of my cap back and showed him a scar about an inch below my hairline where a bull had hooked me my first year riding bulls. It was about four inches long and parallel to my hair.

"That's where he damned near scalped me the first time we met. I was going on kind of like you're doing now. He just reached into his boot and pulled his scalping knife out and started at it. Fortunately, one of his friends stopped him and explained I was just a kid that didn't know no better. He's mellowed some since then, but I wouldn't push it. How long you been here?"

The boy gulped. "About a half hour."

"Yep, that's about how long I'd been there when he pulled the knife."

"Mr. Deerslayer, I'm real sorry. I didn't know. I'll . . . I'll be shutting up now."

The poor boy was so crestfallen that neither I nor J.D. could keep a straight face. Chelsey glared at us both like she was the boy's mother or something. Finally, I couldn't stand it any longer and just burst out laughing. The kid looked up, confused.

"It's okay, son. I was just pulling your leg," I said between laughs. "It's just that you've more than thanked us for that."

"Oh, no, sir. I could never thank you enough."

J.D. jumped in then. "Actually, son, you're right. You can't. That's why cowboys just say thanks, nod their heads, or shake hands when someone saves their lives. They know they can't thank them enough. Now, don't take me wrong. I'm not trying to make us look like heroes. But there's not a guy out there who wouldn't have done the same thing. There were fellas in the arena last night that have saved each of us. And you can't pick them out of the crowd. You know, cowboys have a different idea about gratitude."

"Yeah," I said, "if you can do something for the guy that did something for you, that's fine. But, as often as not, them two fellas split trails right after that, one going north and the other south, heading for different rodeos. So, you might not get the chance to do something for him. Because of that, it's kind of like a tradition to pass on the good deed to someone else. You understand?"

The boy had been silent through the whole thing, but now he nodded. "Yes, sir. At least, I think I do."

"Good. Now, say thanks one last time, shake our hands, and let's go on from there. Okay?"

Again he nodded and reached out his hand for mine. "Thanks, Mr. Carter."

"You're welcome, Jay. And the name is Ira from now on."

"Yes, sir." He reached for J.D.'s hand. "Thanks, Mr. Deerslayer."

"*De nada,* Jay. And call me Johnny."

"Yes, sir."

J.D. and I looked at each other, knowing that customs like "sirring" your elders died hard out in Rocksprings, way out south and west of Llano, where limestone, cedar, and goats were about all a man had to keep him company. The boy had been brought up well.

After we introduced Chelsey, Jay said he had to get on the road. He was headed for South Texas for another rodeo that evening, and he wanted to stop by his home and prove to his mom that he was all right.

"She ain't seen me in nearly three weeks, and she thinks I'm fibbin' to her on the phone when I tell her I'm okay. Besides, she cooks real good."

With that, he said goodbye, tipped his hat to Chelsey, and left. Pretty soon J.D. left, saying he'd see me back at the room later.

"Or maybe not," he added, glancing at Chelsey. For the first time that I could remember, she actually blushed.

After he left, I looked over at Chelsey, but she had her head down, concentrating on her ham and eggs.

"I'm sorry if Johnny embarrassed you, Chelsey. I'm sure he didn't mean any harm."

She looked up at me, not embarrassed in the least. "No, he's fine. I like him."

She finished the last of her toast and leaned forward in her chair, motioning to the waitress for more coffee at the same time. Once our cups were refilled, she looked me hard in the eye.

"You know, if you'd gotten married right out of high school, you could have a kid almost Jay's age now."

I looked up at her, raising one eyebrow in the process. "Oh, yeah? I'd have had to been pretty quick out of the box to do that," I said, a little indignant.

She held up a hand, not one of those manicured, false-nailed ones, but a good, honest working hand, a little rough, but feminine still.

"Hey, I'm not trying to start anything. And I'm not saying you're old. But you're gonna turn thirty-four next year, and you don't even seem to be thinking about the future."

Now I was indignant. "Not thinking about the future? Didn't I go back to school and get a master's degree so I could teach? I know I can't rodeo forever. Hell, I quit riding bulls and broncs five years ago. I still had some good years left for that, but I stopped before I wore myself out and started teaching. I think I got a pretty good future ahead of me, thank you very much."

"You know I'm not talking about that, so quit acting all flustered. You looked pretty good talking to that kid and helping him. I've seen you do it with a lot of the young hands. And I've heard about your classes from a lot of the farm and ranch kids around Waco. They like 'em, say they learn a lot of stuff they never thought would be of any use to 'em. And not just the writing. They say you make them think about things and try to figure them out. You show 'em that an awful lot of complicated things aren't that complicated. Hard, time-consuming, maybe, but not that complicated. You're a good teacher, and you'll make a heck of a father when you decide to finally settle down to it. But sometimes I think somebody has to hit you on the head with a two-by-four to make you look things in the face."

I kind of dropped my head on that one. Chelsey was right.

"I don't know what's going on inside you since Jake died," she continued, "but I can see something happening. I don't know if it's good or bad, but something's going on. I—"

I looked up as a sniff choked off her sentence. She put a sour look on her face and turned her head to one side, but not fast enough for me to miss the sparkles at the corners of her eyes.

"Chelsey, I—"

Her hand came up and shook away my comment. She took a deep breath, looked me in the eyes, and set her mouth straight.

"I don't cry like most girls do, Ira," she said a little shakily. "But, damnit, you sometimes make me just want to bust out in tears."

She had me now. I had no idea what she was talking about. I was completely lost. I'm sure it showed on my face.

"Chelsey, I don't know what to say. I hate to see you cry, but I'll be danged if I know why you're crying."

She nodded, but didn't take her eyes from mine. "Hell, Ira, I'm crying because I love you."

I was dumbfounded. I'd heard the word many times but never thought it quite fit. Right then, it fit perfectly.

"Chelsey, I . . . I . . ."

Again she raised a hand for me to hush. I did.

"I'm not saying it to make you feel awkward or any-thing. It's just that, since Jake died, you've started to act a little different. I know that him being murdered is a hard thing to handle, and I know that you'll do whatever you can to find the man who did it. I think that's what's got me worried.

"You've been awfully quiet, even for you, since his death. Then you disappear for a week or two and I don't even see you or hear from you. Not like I'm some kind of clinging vine. At least, I don't think I am. But I was wor-ried you'd gone and run this guy down. I didn't know if you were dead or alive or wounded or what."

The corner of her eye glistened again, and I felt that glow I'd felt the night before when she'd been so con-cerned about my leg. I reached out and took her hand in mine. I could feel it shaking just the tiniest bit.

"Chelsey, since Jake died, I've had to face some hard facts about myself. I guess I never really thought about dying like I do right now. His was so sudden and out of nowhere. You know, when I step out in the pen each night to do a show, I know there's a chance it could be my last. I know that I might take a hooking or a stomping and die right out there in the dirt in the middle of the arena. But I *know* it's out there. Death just walked in on Jake one sunshiny morning and took him off. He fought it, but it happened. There wasn't anything he could do."

I paused for a second and held her hand tighter.

"Kind of like me, he didn't have a family to speak of. When he died, it made me start to thinking about my life and what I have. And what I don't have. It made me think a lot about me and you. About a family. About the things you're talking about. Once that's over, I want to sit down and talk long and hard with you about the future. But right now, I've got something to do. Maybe by next week . . ."

She looked up at me with eyes sparkling, only partly from the tears, which did their best not to fall from her eyes.

"I can wait, however long it takes. You scare me right now. I can handle your rodeoing. I can handle knowing that you might take a hooking in the pen and not come out. I can handle that. I can even handle whatever it was there in the past that has kept us from talking like this before. But when I saw you again last night, there was a look in your eye, way beyond anything I've ever seen before. I don't know what it is you've got to do this week, but I can handle it, too. It's just that I felt I had to say these things, before it's too late. In case you didn't know. In case you were waiting for me to say them."

I couldn't tear my eyes away from hers. We'd been friends, and more, for a long time. Right then, I felt like I was cheating her—making her wait for something that I thought we both wanted but that might never happen. There were still ghosts from my past. I'd come to grips with most of them, but one remained that kept me from being able to make the commitment that both she and I wanted. I needed time to exorcise the ghost that kept us apart. But first I had to find Jake's killer.

"Give me this week and I'll be able to answer some of your questions—for sure, the most important one. I think you know that I love you, but I do have some things to settle before I'd feel free to act on that. I wouldn't hurt you for the world, and I don't want to build your hopes up, then crash them. I think Jake's death has made me decide to quit waiting around. I don't even know exactly what it is I've been waiting for—a sign from God or what—but I think it may be time to move on. Just give me this week."

Her eyes had never left mine.

"You've got a week, cowboy. But when that week's up, you damn well better take me dancing." She let go of my hand and took a last sip of coffee. "Right now, though, you've got a date with an X-ray machine."

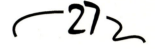

The X-rays showed nothing broken, not even a hairline. Chelsey had to leave right after the Friday night performance to make another show in East Texas, so she wouldn't be staying another night.

Before we left the motel for the rodeo, she dumped the hunter's bags on my bed.

"Make sure that you keep them on right before the rodeo and then during any spots during the perf that you can. You might want to roll one up in a towel and tape it to your leg right before the bull riding to help you get through. But I think you'll live."

That night's bull riding went fine. No big hangups, no hookings. Chelsey paired up with Angie again in the team roping, sitting in second place when the event was over. Angie's husband, Tom, and his partner were in first.

I taped two of the gel packs to my thigh right before the bull riding, wrapped in towels I'd borrowed from the motel. This kept the muscle warm enough and, without any hangups or hookings, I was able to stay in the barrel during the entire bull riding.

After the show, we all went with the rest of the cow-boys and cowgirls to a local joint that gave us a free meal after the rodeo if we showed our association cards. We stayed to ourselves as much as possible, keeping a low profile, blending into the crowd.

About midnight, Chelsey said she had to leave, so J.D. and I took her back to the arena to hook up and head out. Spider nickered as he heard the familiar engine crank up and again when she backed it up to the trailer. He was ready and waiting when she opened the gate of his stall and led him to the trailer. He loaded like a champ.

As she came around the corner of the trailer, I noticed that J.D. had disappeared. It was just Chelsey and me in the moonlight.

I felt bad about letting her leave without giving her a better idea of how I felt about her, but I didn't want to move forward until I knew I'd be around for more than a day or two. After Saturday night, my future might not look too bright.

"Chelsey, I—"

"Shhhh." She put a finger to my lips. Then she pulled herself up on her tiptoes, drew my head down to hers, and kissed me. It was deep and passionate and warm. Every square inch of my lips could feel every bit of hers—every line, every pore. I wanted to stay like that forever, but fi-nally, slowly, we drew apart.

"Don't say anything, Ira," she said as she let her lips leave mine. "I know you. No matter what happens in the next week, I'll know that you are my truest friend. If that's all I ever have from you, it's more than I could ask for. I know you'll do what you think is right, and I respect you for it. Even if it doesn't benefit me. I want to leave you like this, with my name and my kiss on your lips, just in case."

With that, she slipped out of my arms, jumped into the red dually, and pulled smoothly out of the rodeo grounds.

28

The third and final night seemed to take forever. I was glad when the bull riding finally started. I almost blew one of my acts because I was so nervous about the upcoming party. During the cooking act, the bomb button inside the stove seemed to disappear. I found it just as I was thinking I never would. But everything went fine, and we kept the crowd in stitches during the rodeo.

J.D. did a good job fighting bulls that night. Levi Tatum was a new bull rider from Austin whom neither one of us had ever seen before. He was a good hand, but he took a suicide wrap with one of those big, loose-weaved bull ropes. In this wrap, the cowboy weaves the tail in and out of his fingers as he lays the tail in his hand. No matter how hard the bull bucks, it's almost impossible to pull the tail back through the hand, making it a firm "home base" for the bull rider. But that also means it's nearly impossible for the bullfighters to get it loose if the cowboy bucks off before he can undo the wrap.

The Austin cowboy was fine for the first four jumps, his big, black-humped Brahma, Number 26, taking high, easy jumps. On jump five he came around to the right, hard and fast. The limber little twister had him pegged, though, and was sitting perfect for the crackback into his riding hand. The Brahma was bucking high and coming around fast, dropping his front end to put a lot of power into the sudden drop. That usually pulled bull riders down over his head. But not Levi.

Three rounds into the spin, two things happened simultaneously. J.D. moved in closer in anticipation of the whistle, and Levi went to "boot city," spurring the hard-spinning bull with both feet, a strategy to gain points by putting himself in a more precarious position. He got in three good jumps of "two-footin'" before the tooter blew. As soon as the foghorn signaled the end of the ride, J.D. stepped in toward the big bull's head, one hand held out in front of the Brahma's nose to get his attention. As the bull came around, J.D. slapped its nose with his open hand. The bull ignored it. Another round, and J.D. did the same thing. Again, Number 26 took no notice of the bullfighter trying desperately to get his attention.

Levi had stopped spurring and had reached down for his tail. It is the cowboy's job to unwrap the tail of the rope from around his hand before trying to get off the bull, if at all possible. If he doesn't, the getaway isn't clean and he could be "hung up," unable to get loose. Levi had reached for his tail and had it in his hand. One more jump and he would have pulled it, waited for a good jump, and bailed off, clean and easy. But he never got that next jump.

Just as Levi's hand grabbed the tail, the big Brahma's leading foot slipped out from under him and the animal went to his knees. He was up again in a split-second, but it was enough of a jolt to throw Levi down on the black hump and cause him to lose hold with his spurs. The bull's head came up and a horn caught the cowboy right above his left eye. The little bull rider was knocked out cold, and his hand fell away from the tail of his bull rope.

I was out of the barrel the second the bull stumbled, even though my leg was still stiff and sore. I waited as the bull came toward me, but he was too intent on dumping the limp package attached to his side. On each jump he'd hook back with a pair of eight-inch gray-and-black-striped horns and pop Levi with them. Levi was a sack of old laundry, arms and legs flailing from the centrifugal force, only to be stopped each time with a thump of the horns. Fortunately, he was wearing a protective vest, but his head, arms, legs, and pelvis were vulnerable targets.

I saw J.D. on the other side actually grab the bull's head with both hands, but he wasn't able to get a good hold. The big, black, snot-blowing head came back around to my side, and I ignored it except to get the timing down. As it passed by, I stepped in, aiming for the shoulder following it and trying to press my body in as close as possible to the bull's. I was inside the arc of his head, and his body hadn't come around yet to knock me down. Now I was between the bull's horns and Levi, right where I wanted to be. As the bull's front feet hit the ground, the rider's hung hand was at its lowest point. I reached up and put both hands on top of the bull's back, trying hard to catch sight of the bull rope's handhold inside all the dust and snot and sweat. I saw it and grabbed for it, and was rewarded with the feel of Levi's arm under mine. I clamped onto his arm and what I could get of the handhold, like a drowning man grabbing a life preserver.

The bull went up in the front end then, taking both me and Levi with him. The whole time he was going up, my eyes were glued to the spot where Levi's hand and the bull rope met. My right hand was holding Levi's hand and my left one found the rope tail. I jerked hard and felt it come loose a little, probably popping one finger out. About then, the bull hit the ground with a grinding impact that shook my teeth. I pulled again and felt another satisfying little give in the tail as another finger came loose.

Just then, something caught me in the back of the head. An explosion of red and orange blocked out all vision, and, from a brain center somewhere in the depths of consciousness, I got a message telling me I'd been hooked in the back of the head. I felt Levi's arm slipping away, and there was nothing I could do about it. The bull's body, Levi's chaps, and a pair of boots with spurs flooded over me and rolled me like a twig in a tsunami. I hit on my back and rolled, came up on my feet, and shook my head to clear my eyesight.

The bull was spinning away from me and going up again. Just barely, I could see J.D.'s hat and one arm in the same place I had been but from the opposite side. Somehow, he'd gotten into the well, or the inside of the spin, and was in there untying Levi's hand. Ol' 26 hit the ground again with his head pointed my way, only about three feet away. I leaned in and slapped him on the nose. This time he turned toward me. I planted my left foot and went right. Out of the corner of my eye, I saw J.D. give a final pull. The tail came loose in his hand, and Levi's arm slid from view as he came loose. Problem now was that my current path would take the bull right back over him.

With my left hand on the bull's head for reference, I stuck my left foot in the sand and turned to my right again, leaving my back an open target to the Brahma until I got turned all the way around and found him with my right hand. I felt him snuffin' at me as I made the pivot and felt his massive head hook at that left hand. When he did that, I let go and completed the pivot, bringing my right hand around to slap him, if necessary. But his hooking charge carried him just far enough to allow my pivot to put me right at his right shoulder. Fortunately, I hadn't crossed feet or anything during the whole process, and I came out alive. I pushed off his head with my right hand and let him go blowing by me.

Two cowboys hauled Levi out of the way as J.D. and I

stood side by side, feet planted and arms bent just above waist level between the cowboy and the bull. But 26 had had enough excitement for the night and ambled nonchalantly through the let-out gate on the opposite side of the arena.

J.D. and I each let out a deep breath, almost as one. He held his hand out high above his head, and I gave him a big high-five. The adrenaline pump started to back off a little, and I could see him visibly relax. I felt the same subtle letdown, but almost immediately there was a sharp pain at the back of my head. I must have winced because J.D. motioned for me to turn around. I twisted my head and heard him whistle.

"Good one, Ira."

As I reached back to feel, J.D. caught my hand with his.

"Nope, pard. You ain't putting that nasty, grungy, bullshit-covered hand back there on an open wound," he said, and motioned for the Justin Healer to come my way. "You just asking to get a brain infection or something?"

The Justin doc hauled me behind the chutes to clean the wound. He stuck a bandage over it and made me promise to get stitches after the rodeo. I promised, but kept my fingers crossed. It wasn't like it was on my beautiful mug or anything, so I figured I'd just keep the bandage on it and let it heal. I'd go to the doctor if it looked like it wasn't healing right.

The doc told me that Levi was fine. He'd been popped above the eye and knocked out. When he came to behind the chutes, he didn't remember a thing after the whistle. Had a headache was all, he said.

Just then, they announced that Levi had scored an 89 to move him into the lead in the bull riding event.

The next-to-last bull rider was Frankie Armstrong. I tried to keep my mind on my job, but it was hard. His bull bucked all right, but nothing spectacular. He spun to the left, but he was pretty slow. Jake could have ridden him.

I was interested in seeing how this would play out. The ride was worth maybe an 85, possibly 86 or 87, but it just wasn't the ride that Levi had made.

Ray got the score from the man who tallied both of the judge's scores. I saw a brief frown cross his face.

"Ladies and gentlemen, a new leader in the bull riding. Frankie Armstrong marks a 90 on that ride to move into the lead for the bullriding event."

I saw Ray look over at one of the judges in disgust. I followed his gaze. Over near the let-out gate, Frankie was slapping judge Harvey Colburn on the back. I made a mental note to check into Harvey's background when I got back home—if I got back home.

The last bull bucked, throwing his rider before the whistle and leaving Frankie as the Llano bullriding champion.

29

As the last bull left the ring, J.D. and I headed for the truck. I was rolling my barrel away from the let-out gate and J.D. was walking alongside when a voice called out. "Ira!"

I turned to see Andy Tetracini and Frankie Armstrong headed toward us.

"Long time no see, son," Andy said as he got close, stopping and giving a big bear hug. He must have been at least seventy years old, but he was still a strong man. He'd been a steer wrestler and saddle bronc rider when he'd ridden with Jake in the old days.

"Too long, Mr. Tetracini," I said, hugging him back for survival's sake. He stopped his hugging long enough to push me away and hold me at arm's length in those big bear paws he called hands.

"Mr. Tetracini? Jake, may he rest in peace, was like a brother to me. You were like a son to him. You know what that makes you? Like a nephew to me. You call me Andy or I'll turn you over my knee."

Andy smiled and I had to smile back. I couldn't believe

this man had killed Jake or had Jake killed. The two had always cared for each other. Despite his size and strength, he had always been a gentle man. I'd never heard of him hurting anyone. The mob makes sure you never see them do it, of course, but I'd been in newspapers for several years before going to work for the magazine and my contacts would have let me know if they'd heard anything like that. Jake had told me how Andy had really tried to embody the cowboy spirit. He'd always held to that ambiguous, hard-to-grasp cowboy "code" that civilians always talked about but rarely understood. He had his own code of ethics and a firm belief in right and wrong. J.D. told me that Andy had gone back to the mob when his father died and left him as the only son to take care of an aging mother and two younger sisters.

"He was a knight born in the wrong time, a cowboy like you see in the movies," Jake had told J.D. "Even in the mob business, he played fair. Always fair."

"Ira, you remember Frankie, don't you?"

Andy let go of my right shoulder long enough to pull Frankie forward. Frankie hadn't aged well. He was only a year or two older than me—thirty-five, maybe thirty-six. But he looked older, at least in his late forties. He still dressed well, even in cowboy clothes. He wore the nearly regulation Wranglers and a cowboy shirt required by the association, but his Wranglers were tailored and his shirts were custom-made with his brand monogramed tastefully on the left chest pocket flap, where most folks had their initials. His hat wasn't the standard 4X Resistol; it was hand-made in Wyoming and at least a 10X, if not a 20. His boots, custom-fitted and personalized, probably cost at least $1,000. He was still in shape, with a narrow waist, wide shoulders, and thigh muscles threatening to flatten the crease of his starched jeans. But his face had seen better days. Wrinkles were set deep in his eyes, and he was starting to get jowls, fleshy cheeks, and a double chin. His graying hair had lost some of its shine.

J.D. had told me that Frankie had picked up the same desire to be a cowboy that his father had, but not for the same reasons. He liked the fame, the machismo that went with being a cowboy. He was more of the brawler, chauvinistic to a fault, and he loved to hurt people. He'd been fined and blacklisted more than once for being cruel to the animals he'd drawn. The association had thrown him out, supposedly for life, after he'd killed a barrel racer's horse with a steel pipe at the Chicago rodeo. The barrel racer had refused to go to bed with him, so he'd beaten her up, raped her. Then he'd dragged her to the door of the dressing room of her horse trailer so she could see him kill her horse. When Andy found out about it, he paid for the girl's medical bills, some shrink work, and bought her another, better horse. He'd also put a down payment on a little ranch outside her hometown for her. Now she was a top contender for the world every year, having come in second at last year's world championship. Two years after the incident, Frankie bought his way back into the association.

He didn't reach out a hand to shake. He just stared at me, his eyes burning into mine. If the anger hadn't been forcing me to play it cool, I'd have probably given him a "go-to-hell" look right back. Instead, I smiled and nodded politely.

"Frankie, good to see you. Nice ride tonight. You end up winning a second?"

Frankie's eyes burned deeper into mine, maybe catching the intended slur.

"First. I always win first."

Wrong, I thought, *you always buy first,* but I let it slide.

"Well," Andy broke in, "you coming up to the party?"

"Wouldn't miss it for the world," I answered, not taking my eyes from Frankie's. "I hope you got a place we can

George Wilhite 127

clean up there. I'd hate to miss any of the action by going back to the motel to get all this gunk off."

"Not a problem," Andy said. "Come on up. I've got a whole suite you boys can have for the night. Bathroom bigger than your whole motel room."

He laughed, slapped Frankie on the back, and started off. Frankie and I stood eye to eye for a moment longer before he stalked off after his father without another word.

30

Before we left, I reached behind the seat of my truck and pulled out my old Colt revolver. I stuck it in my bag underneath the blank pistol and a couple of left-over bombs, and carefully set the bag between us in the front seat.

I let J.D. drive out to the hideaway, as he knew the way. We left the main highway a couple of miles out of town and crossed the Llano River, its winding course visible as a silver strand that wound its way through piles of black masses in the river bed—black masses that the morning sun would turn back into normal red-sand-colored boulders and light-green willows and mesquites. It was beautiful country but desolate and lonely until modern transportation and good roads brought folks closer together—closer, that is, in travel time, not necessarily closer in true distance. Even with all the modern roads, cars, and trucks, the Llano occasionally went on a rampage that played havoc with asphalt roads and smaller bridges, so that one-hour trips to town became all-day outings. Sometimes it was just plain impossible to get across the river, and residents were stranded on one side or the other.

J.D. broke me out of my dream state with a pointed reminder.

"Remember, we have to find the disk the story is on before we can do anything else. We have to have that story to back up our play."

I shifted in my seat and we talked for a few minutes until we both felt comfortable with the plan. We would find the disk, then see if there was any evidence that might lead us to Jake's killer. J.D. seemed to think that the killer might even be staying at the hideaway.

"This is one of the places they used to send folks who needed to 'disappear' right after a job, whether it was a big robbery, a drug deal, or a murder. No one sees you out here, and there's enough open space to make that a permanent situation, if necessary. There's a body or two buried out here amongst the mesquites and rocks."

He turned to me, his face glowing a funny green from the dash lights reflecting off his grease paint makeup.

"What's the deal with you and the lady horse doctor?"

"What do you mean?"

"Y'all getting hitched or anything?"

I thought about it a minute before I answered. "No. Why?"

J.D. cast another sidelong glance at me, holding a few seconds before looking back to the road. "Yeah, you've got me convinced. Well, one of the best shots we'll have is to pick up one or two of the women there and make for a bedroom. That happens all night long out here. If we can pick up two as soon as we get in, they'll provide us with a cover for being missing. It shouldn't be too hard. They all think bullfighters are the best of cowboys and professional athletes all rolled into one. I just didn't know if that might be a problem for you, what with the lady doc and all."

I could feel my face blushing, but I knew he couldn't see it under the red and white makeup.

"No. I've got some things to work out before I'm free to even think about that. We talked about it a little, but I need to clear something up in my mind."

I looked out the window at the shadows and moonlight before continuing.

"There was a girl once. Things didn't work out, but it wasn't her fault or mine. I keep wondering if I'm over her."

J.D. looked as closely at me as he could while paying attention to the paved ranch road that wandered between truck-sized rocks and an occasional tree.

"What happened? Or do you not want to talk about it?"

I shrugged. "No big deal. I met a gal at a rodeo once. A spectator. Not a buckle bunnie, or a groupie or some dim-witted blonde that didn't have enough sense to come in out of the rain. She was class. I saw her sitting in the stands, and made sure that one of my acts took me close to her. She didn't have a ring on, so I figured she was fair game. I was wrong. We met a couple of times while the rodeo was in town, but her family took offense. Felt I was beneath her. Sent her brother around to warn me off when the rodeo was over."

J.D. continued to scrutinize me. "I never knew you to back off because some big lug told you to."

It was more of a question than a statement.

"He had help—enough that I figured they could keep us apart and make things miserable for her if I didn't go along."

"Knowing you, that would have to be some big help."

"It was." I paused before I dropped the bomb on J.D. "Her brother was Frankie Armstrong."

31

He took it better than I thought he would. His right leg went rigid against the brake, the truck swerved off the shoulder, and we came to rest with the right front tire only about a foot from a prickly pear that was starting to bloom. It only took about a minute before he finally started breathing normally again, but I thought the shock must have done something to his vocal cords. He couldn't complete a sentence.

"You—you mean—but Andy . . ."

There wasn't enough room in the truck cab for his arms to move like he wanted, flailing the air like that, so he opened the door and stepped out where he had room to flail away. He stopped ten feet away, only to return and stick his head back in the open door. "Alisa . . . Alisa?"

I nodded.

His eyes rolled in his head as he slapped his forehead. "Oh, Jesus Christ. Oh, Lord Almighty. Oh, God."

I knew he wasn't addressing me, but I spoke up anyway as I got out and moved to the driver's side of the pickup. "J.D., look, I know I should have said—"

He turned back to me, looking as if I were a vampire or something. "*Said* something? *Said* something? You get warned off a Mafia princess by her brother, who likes to eat people for breakfast, and you think you should have *said* something? You should have said *plenty,* and a long time ago! I can't believe you didn't tell me."

He swung in a big circle with his arms spread wide, looking at the moon and moving his lips in a silent moan, before walking back to me with his head shaking back and forth.

"Why?" he asked, his eyes raised to mine.

I ducked my eyes away from his.

"I didn't know anything about the mob until you told me in Espanola. I'd always thought the part about Andy was a joke of Jake's, and I thought Frankie just had a bunch of despicable friends, enough of them to waste me in an alley somewhere and make life miserable for Alisa. But I had no idea they were mob-related. Hell, they were involved in rodeo, how could they be in the mob?"

J.D. didn't panic easily, but he had a right to tonight, I realized.

"When I did realize the Mafia was involved and who Andy and Frankie were, I had to know if Alisa knew anything about it. I loved her. I think I still do, but I have to know. Besides, you saw how Frankie reacted. He hates me. He loathes me. He was concentrating so hard on me that you could have been wearing a cop's uniform or an FBI vest and he would never have noticed you. Me being here has thrown him off balance. He's just a hair uncertain, but he would never dream that we're here for anything other than the rodeo. He doesn't know I know about his mob connection. But my presence will upset him enough that he probably won't ever recognize you, especially if we can get you in a room with some girl as soon as we get there. By the way, what does Linda think about you picking up some woman at this party?"

George Wilhite 133

J.D. finally returned to normal and smiled thinly.

"She's got no problem with it. She knows I'm not here to get laid or have a good time. She knows I'm only here to get Jake's killer. She also knows I'll do whatever it takes."

His jaw had taken that determined set again. I put my hand on his shoulder. "Does she know that she may never see you again?"

"Yeah," he said, slowly nodding his head, then looking back into my eyes, "if that's what it takes."

Approaching car lights caught my eye. A large, white luxury car gleamed in reflected moonlight as it wound its way up the ranch road toward us and the hideaway beyond. I looked back at J.D.

"I'll do everything I can to make sure that's not what it takes."

The car pulled and stopped abreast of our truck. J.D. was climbing into the truck cab as the window on the passenger side rolled down. I started toward the car but stopped when Frankie's face filled the open window.

"Trouble?" he sneered at me.

I threw a big smile back at him. "Naw, damn jackrabbit. I never can bring myself to hit 'em. Swerved and almost blew a tire on a prickly pear. Just got out to make sure there was no damage."

Frankie looked me up and down with that glaring smirk of his. "Yeah, you always was soft."

"Frankie," Andy called sharply from the unseen back of the limousine, "you shut up."

The rear window on the passenger's side rolled down to reveal Andy's white-haired head. He grinned at me.

"If your truck is okay, fall in behind us and follow us up to the house. It's party time," he said.

I grinned back at him and said something about us being ready, but I don't even remember what. My heart had taken leave. When I'd dipped down to talk to him, I'd seen a glimpse of her. There was no mistake. Her ivory skin stood out of the darkness of the interior even more because of the frame of long, straight black hair. She looked just like she had in Chicago, that night in the stands. She'd stood out in a crowd of five thousand other people; she'd surely stand out in a carful of four. And I'd heard her slight intake of breath and seen her hand go to her mouth. She'd recognized me.

Andy's window raised with the little whine of an electronic motor, shutting off my view of her before I could bend lower to see the rest of her face. It was probably a good thing. I don't know if I could have kept a straight face or not.

Back in the truck, J.D. was waiting for me with a question.

"Does Andy know?"

"I don't know," I said truthfully as I put the truck in gear and followed the limo. "He might. He might not. I saw him a bunch of times after that at some of the big East Coast rodeos, but he never said anything. That's one reason I never made the connection between Frankie and Alisa and him."

J.D. contemplated that. "I'd think that if he knew and he disapproved, you would have known."

I turned sharply toward him. "You don't mean—"

"I mean either he doesn't know, or he knows and he approves."

"But if her family had Jake murdered?"

"Love don't give a shit about family, Ira. If she had nothing to do with it . . ."

He left it unfinished.

32

We pulled into the hideaway just a few seconds behind Andy and Frankie. I caught a brief glimpse of
Alisa being hustled into the massive mahogany front
doors. I'd expected a fortress, but the hideaway looked
like any run-of-the-mill millionaire's mansion. The huge
wooden doors, decorated with beveled, leaded glass, glistened like crystal from the interior lights. Leading up to
the doors, a row of white and gray marble steps nearly as
long as a football field lifted the house a good fifteen feet
above the driveway. At the top of the steps, a deep porch
of the same marble supported towering white columns
that reached two stories before providing the foundation
for a verandah, where the bulk of the guests seemed to be
spilling out of French doors.

But instead of the faint clicking of champagne glasses
and hushed social talk you would expect to find at such a
site, loud voices and guffawing filled the star-studded
night air. Cowboys whose jeans still carried the sweaty
hair of bulls or broncs worked their way around the tuxe-
doed and evening-gowned crowd that had shown up from

New York and L.A. and other citadels of civilization for a peek at this wild side of humanity. As I looked up at the balcony, stocky little bulldogger "Crazy Bill" Snodgrass held a laughing New York debutante upside down over the railing with one hand while explaining the intricacies of her lace thong underwear to one of the less socially enlightened bronc riders. When Crazy Bill asked her if he could have them for a souvenir, she nodded somewhere under the upside-down expanse of her evening dress. He was in the process of removing them when he glanced down and saw me coming up the steps.

"Ira Carter! You ol' son of a bitch! Get your ass up here and help us out. It's getting too damn quiet around here."

With a deft movement of his free hand, Bill snatched the panties from between the girl's legs before lifting her back over the railing and setting her, still upside down, inelegantly on the floor. The young bronc rider moved eagerly to assist her to an upright position as Bill headed toward the stairs to meet us.

Crazy Bill had gotten his name from pulling these same kinds of antics consistently during his career. He was from some little hole-in-the-wall up near the Arctic Circle in Canada and had never quite figured out social niceties. The first time anyone ever saw him was ten years ago at Tulsa, where he'd made the record books by throwing his steer in 3.9 seconds (a full second faster than anyone else there) by literally leaping from his horse across six or seven feet of space. Most steer wrestlers rode in close, dropped down from a couple of feet away, and then scientifically pulled their steers to the ground by utilizing the steer's own momentum and a leverage-producing hold on its nose. But Bill thought nothing of jumping across space to reach his steer faster, then throwing all science to the wind to drop his steer by sheer strength. That same year, he became the first cowboy to ride his steer wrestling horse up the elevator of the Tulsa hotel that served as rodeo headquarters. He'd charged into the ballroom during the big awards banquet and dance after the rodeo, and swooped up the shy little barrel racer that he'd set his eye on at the beginning of the rodeo. Unfortunately, her dad and four brothers were also there. They stopped Bill, hog-tied him, and left him in the broom closet of the penthouse ballroom. The next morning they let him out and they all went to breakfast. Nobody ever stayed mad at Bill for long.

Bill stormed down the stairs and wrapped me in a bear hug with his massive arms. He was so short, though, that his arms only came to my waist.

"Goddamn, Ira, I ain't seen you in three or four years. I didn't know you were clowning this rodeo. I just got here in time to run my steer, then we loaded up and come up here. Where the hell you been?"

I extracted myself as best I could from Bill's arms and tried to draw a breath through the bruised-if-not-broken ribs he often left in the wake of his hugs. I noticed that J.D. had withdrawn into the edge of the surrounding crowd, far enough to be out of range of Bill's exuberance but close enough to follow me.

"I've been teaching, down at the college in Hillsboro," I finally managed to say.

"Teaching? That's a hell of an occupation for a damn good cowboy. But I guess it's better than clerking."

Bill grabbed me by the elbow and led me, with J.D. following, into the assembly of cowboys, cowgirls, dandies, and debutantes. He squinted with his head stuck out in front of him, looking around like he'd lost somebody—first to the left, then to the right, then stopping and looking behind us as if somebody might be sneaking up on us.

"Now, Ira, I seen a pretty little filly right around this here area a minute ago, just your type, I bet. Looked smart, real smart—not just that stupid, silly, social smart you see in most gals these days. Now where in the hell did she—"

He stopped in midstep and turned to look up into my face.

"I'm sorry, Ira. I never asked. You married or anything?"

I had to smile. Bill had married his shy little barrel racer a year or so after sweeping her off her feet in Tulsa, but it hadn't slowed him down. The only difference was that everyone knew Bill drew the line well before anything ever happened. Pulling panties off a girl at a rodeo party was one thing; cheating on little Taylor Marie Goodwin Snodgrass was another. All in all, she put up with his carrying on as long as he could look her in the face when he came home. Bill was a wild and crazy cowboy, but he couldn't lie worth a shit. And we all knew that he loved Taylor Marie more than anything else in the world. Except maybe rodeo and rodeo parties.

"No, Bill, I ain't married or nothing."

With a whoop, he turned again and started stalking through the crowd. Suddenly, he let out another yell and steered me off to the right. "There she is. Pretty thing." He winked up at me with a big grin. "I'd run her myself if I was ten years younger and single. But I ain't, so I guess you can have a shot at her."

Just then, we pulled up to a mixed group of cowboys and dudes, and Bill sort of just bulled his way into the middle. J.D. continued to follow, but hung back in the crowd.

"Young lady, I'd like to introduce you to my very best friend in the whole wide world and probably the most eligible bachelor ever known to man, Ira Carter."

I hadn't quite fit through Bill's hole in the outer circle, so I couldn't see the vision of loveliness he had chosen for me, but I figured it would work into our plan pretty well. A final tug on my arm popped me through the two huge gorilla-looking dudes that Bill had just pushed so easily aside. I turned my head aside to nod and mumble a polite "sorry" before looking at my date for the night.

"Ira, I'd like you to meet—" He paused, waiting for her name.

"Alisa . . ." she said. "Alisa Tetracini."

Leave it to Bill to pick Alisa out of the whole group. She was looking me square in the eyes, not a feather ruffled. I nodded my head toward her.

"Pleased . . . pleased to meet you, Miss Tetracini."

"Well, I'll leave you two lovebirds alone while I go back to partying a little bit. You treat Ira right, Miss Tetraninny. He's my very best friend."

I stood speechless, my heart pounding and sending huge globules of blood through my system until they got to my head, where they found it nearly impossible to get through the arteries and veins. It felt like each pulse was sending a golf ball to my head.

Alisa smiled down at Bill.

"I'll try to make sure he's none the worse for wear, sir."

As she turned to me, the golf balls grew to softball size in their fight to pass through the arteries on the sides of my head. The rest of the room blurred as her face came into focus. I was growing hot and couldn't seem to catch my breath.

"Ira."

"Alisa." I stammered it out, feeling my tongue swollen and cottony in my mouth as I said it, but the word itself came out like liquid gold, smooth as silk.

She was just the way I'd last seen her: perfect white face with its small turned-up nose and naturally pink lips. She'd never worn lipstick; she didn't need it. Her brown eyes glittered with flecks of green. Her eyelashes were long and silky, no mascara needed. Her hair was pulled back with a clasp at the back of her neck, where it then flowed down her back to her waist. Her white shoulders sloped invitingly into a blue satin evening gown, its bodice pointing to a patch of cleavage more sensed than seen. With every breath, the gown shimmered and moved.

"It's been a long time," I finally managed.

"Too long," she responded, reaching out her hand to take mine.

Turning, she introduced me to the crowd, but I didn't hear anyone's name. I nodded as I heard the mumble of her speech.

"Ira and I are old friends, from way back," she concluded.

I looked at her to see how she meant it. She looked straight back at me and smiled a perfect smile that told me she meant it.

"Now, if you'll excuse me, Ira and I have a lot to catch up on."

The two gorillas moved to go with her, but a slight movement of her hand dismissed them.

"We'll be in the study, if my father is looking for me."

33

I didn't know what to expect. It had been years since we'd seen each other. She raised an eyebrow as J.D. followed along.

"It's okay. He's my partner."

She nodded slightly, then led the way through the throng of guests and down a side hallway until the three of us stood before a set of double doors. She looked both ways before she silently slid the doors apart and motioned us to enter. Turning to us, she put her forefinger in front of her luscious lips, rolled her eyes to indicate the entire room, and mouthed the word "bugged." Walking briskly to the fireplace on the opposite wall, she pressed some hidden catch, and a hidden panel in the mantel opened to reveal a set of switches. She pressed one, then returned to us, visibly relaxed.

"The whole place is bugged," she said, moving to my side and whispering. "But this is Dad's study, his only private place in the whole house, so he had a device installed, unknown to Frankie, to jam the bugs. Something about playing a tape of normal room noises on the frequency of the bugs so that it sounds like the room is empty. We can talk here."

"Alisa, I—"

She put her finger to my lips this time.

"You don't have to tell me. I picked up enough from snatches of conversation between Frankie and his goons to get a good idea of what was going on. One of them said that you didn't even flinch until they told you how they could make life miserable for me. I also know you didn't take the money they offered you."

She smiled for a moment.

"Gordo, the big one, was really mad when you threw the money in his face. He wanted to hurt you then. Probably still does. But that doesn't tell me why you're here tonight. I assume it wasn't to see me. There were easier and better ways to do that."

I looked at J.D. He nodded one short, curt nod. "Tell her. It's the only way to find out," he said.

I turned back to Alisa. "Jake Lawson was killed a couple of weeks ago."

Her eyes never left mine as she nodded. "I heard. Dad was terribly upset. He wanted to go to the funeral, but the shock of it caused a mild seizure and his doctor wouldn't let him go."

I raised my eyebrow at that. She nodded slightly.

"I know. He looks healthy as a horse, but he's not well. The doctor's say that an extreme shock could kill him. Jake's death had him bed-ridden for almost a week. He's only just gotten back up again."

"Well, Jake's death is why we're here. Jake was murdered. Because of a story he was going to write. He was going to expose what he knew about the mob connection in rodeo. We think the mob had him killed."

She took a step back from me then.

"You don't mean you think Dad had anything to do with it, do you?"

I shook my head. "No, but we think Frankie might."

She looked puzzled. "But Dad and Jake go back a long way. Why would Jake suddenly decide to do a piece on the mob? He would have known how much trouble it would bring him."

"Because of me." J.D. stepped forward. "I think you're legit, so I'm going to tell you. If it gets out, you're the only who knows. I'll come back for you if that happens."

Alisa looked at J.D. and nodded seriously. "I believe you would. Your secret will be safe with me."

J.D. then proceeded to tell her his story, focusing on the part about Frankie wanting to force him back into working for the mob.

"And Ira parted company with Frankie on pretty bad terms, too. Whoever killed Jake took the disk that had the story on it. It was the only one he had. He didn't dare leave a hard copy out anywhere."

"And you thought whoever killed Jake might be hiding out here? No one new has come in since Jake's death. Do you know what the disk looks like?"

I shook my head, but J.D. nodded.

"I snuck back to see Jake a month or so before he was killed. He showed it to me, put it in the computer and let me read it to see if everything was correct. It's a floppy. Red with a black and white label. He had written 'Down Payment' on it with a black felt-tip pen."

Alisa took a deep breath. Her shoulders drooped a little, and she pressed her lips together tightly as she looked at the floor. Then she raised her head, and I saw a tiny tear escape from the corner of her left eye.

"Follow me. I think I know where it is."

34

We didn't go by way of the hall this time. Alisa walked up to a section of the wall paneling and reached under the moulding. There was a faint click and the panel slid away, exposing a passageway. She motioned for us to follow as she stepped into the hidden hall.

"You can't expect a mob hideaway not to have secret passageways, can you?"

We followed the hidden tunnel for only a short way before Alisa stopped, put her ear to the wall, and listened. Nodding to us, she pressed another hidden button that opened a door into another office. Again she put her forefinger to her mouth to signal us to silence and mouthed the words "Frankie's office."

Inside, she went directly to his desk and quietly opened the top right-hand drawer. She took out a disk and handed it to me, then motioned us back to the passageway. Wanting to be sure it was the right disk, I turned back toward the desk and reached for the lamp switch. For the first time, I realized I was still carrying my gear bag with all my clowning stuff inside. I set it down beside the desk.

Everything seemed to happen at once when I flipped on the lamp switch. I heard a faint, pleading "No" from Alisa and looked up just long enough to see her already in the passageway with her hand outstretched toward me as the secret panel started to slide closed. That same instant, I heard the door to the room open, and I swiveled around just in time to see Frankie and Andy step into the room.

Frankie was on me in a second. I smashed a fist into his face and had the satisfaction of feeling his nose break.

As Frankie fell back on his butt, two of his mobsters rushed through the door. The closest one pulled a gun and snapped a shot off at me. I heard it cut hairs on the side of my head, but otherwise it thunked harmlessly into the wall behind me. Before he could get off a second shot, Andy stepped in front of him, his opened hand in front of the thug's eyes.

"Stop!"

It was an order, with the unflinching authority of years behind it. The thug didn't pull the trigger, but he kept the pistol leveled at me in case I gave him an excuse to use it. I didn't plan on doing that. What I did was try to palm as much as possible of the disk and push it up my left sleeve. I got most of it up there, but I had to keep my hand curled slightly to keep it from dropping back out. Fortunately, it was small enough to hide in my cuff.

The second thug helped Frankie up from the carpet. I could feel the hate shooting from his eyes as he stepped toward me, his broken nose sitting a little to the left. He sniffed, trying to stop the blood from oozing, and pushed his helper away.

"Get me some gauze from the medicine cabinet," he barked.

While the mobster headed for a first-aid kit, Andy kept himself between Frankie and me, his back at first toward me but then turning to look me in the eyes, one hand behind him holding Frankie back.

"You wanna explain to me what you're doing in Frankie's office?"

"I was looking for a place to change. Must've taken a wrong turn."

"Where's your friend, the bullfighter?"

It suddenly dawned on me that I hadn't seen J.D. since the door opened. I tried to concentrate with my peripheral vision without moving my eyes, but I couldn't see him anywhere in the room.

"I don't know. I think he got hooked up with some girl and moseyed off looking for a quiet place, if you know what I mean."

"If that's all you were doing, why did you hit Frankie?"

I looked at Frankie standing behind his father, as he always had—using his dad's standing in the mob as leverage to get away with things the organization would never have allowed of anyone else. *The old man doesn't even know how bad Frankie is,* I thought. As that thought flickered through my head, I caught a subtle movement by the door, behind the huge gorilla with the gun aimed at the bridge of my nose. From behind the massive office door, slung open by the two thugs when they rushed in, J.D. stuck his orange-wigged head out, peeked around, and winked at me. I looked back at Andy.

"He rushed me. I didn't even know who it was until after I hit him. I hit anybody who looks like they're gonna lay a hand on me."

"He's lying, Papa. He was in here snooping."

Andy took the restraining hand off Frankie's right arm and held it up slightly behind his shoulder. "Quiet. I'm asking the questions."

"But Papa . . ."

Andy turned and grabbed Frankie by the shoulders, shaking him. "I told you to be quiet."

Something must have snapped in Frankie. Maybe it was the pain from the broken nose. More likely, it was the humiliation of being knocked on his rump by a guy in baggy pants, a red wig, and clown makeup. And right in his own office.

With an animal-like roar, he knocked his father aside and lunged at me. I tried to block his attack, but I had to use my left hand. When I moved it, the disk flew out, landing in front of Andy on the floor. I saw him pick it up as I went down under Frankie's rush. Some of the blood from his broken nose got in my eye as I went down and I couldn't see much, but I could see enough to catch him right on the nose again. It was a solid right jab that closed his eyes for a second and made him go limp. But not for long. He got on top of me and caught both my arms against my side with his knees. His face seethed with anger, and bloody bubbles formed in his nose as he cussed and slobbered above me. His right hand went back, and I tried to come up with a way to avoid it.

Suddenly, the look in Frankie's eyes changed. Surprise registered, but I didn't know why. I looked up at his right hand to see a massive fist locked around his wrist. Then I heard a dull thud. Frankie's eyes closed again, and as he fell to one side I could see J.D. standing behind him with one hand letting go of his wrist and the other holding a .45 automatic. Behind him, the thug who'd shot at me lay full length on the carpet, a hefty cast-iron Chinese dog bookend beside his head, covered with blood.

35

We helped Andy off the floor to the chair behind the desk. J.D. heaved Frankie onto the leather sofa, then turned back to the desk, stuffing the .45 into the pocket of his baggies.

Andy sat with his head slumped, holding the disk in one hand. I raised one leg and sat on the desk, to his left and facing him. Slowly he raised his head and looked at me. With an aged hand, he held up the disk. "What's this?"

Before I could answer, a moan escaped from the couch. Frankie's hand went to his head, his eyes opened, and he sat up. As soon as he did, his other hand went to his nose.

"Ohhh!"

"Maybe you ought to ask Frankie," I said, nodding at Andy's worse-for-wear son. "It came from his desk."

The old man straightened up and, with a voice that had some of its authority back, addressed his offspring.

"What do you know about this, Frankie?"

Frankie dropped his hands to his knees, but his face remained contorted. Not in pain this time. In hate.

"It's a story that son-of-a-bitch friend of yours was going to run about Mafia involvement in rodeo. I got it from him."

I hadn't expected it to be that easy. Andy dropped his eyes, but only for a second. "Then you . . ."

"Yeah, I killed the old fart. He was going to expose our operation. I couldn't let him."

Andy's face grew tight. His eyes narrowed. "But he was our friend. He could have done this years ago. He never did. What makes you think he would do so now?"

Frankie grinned evilly and flipped a hand carelessly toward me. "Ask your 'practically a nephew' there. He knows."

Andy looked at me. I pointed at J.D.

"Look familiar?"

Andy shook his head. J.D. took off his wig, undid the yellow bandanna from around his neck, and used it to wipe off most of the grease paint from his face. For the first time since we'd arrived at the rodeo, he let the fake hillbilly clown voice drop and used his own.

"Hello, Uncle Andy."

Andy's voice trembled. "J.D.? Is that you?"

J.D. nodded and stepped closer to the desk, crossing in front of the now closed doors. Andy stood halfway up, reaching one arm out to J.D.

"We thought you were dead, even your father. What—"

He didn't get to finish the question. The thug who'd gone for bandages slung the door open and stepped inside the room, carrying a tray with water and assorted first-aid items on it. With his free right hand, he closed the door and stepped between Frankie and J.D.

At that instant, Frankie flashed off the couch and grabbed the thug, reaching inside his coat for the automatic he carried in a shoulder holster. J.D., seeing the weapon, pulled the .45 out of his baggies and fired. The bullet caught the thug square in the chest, knocking him backward. Frankie ducked to the floor off to one side and tore off a shot at J.D., catching him in the shoulder and spinning him around. The champ dropped his pistol.

While all that was going on, I dropped behind the desk and grabbed my gear bag, pulling it behind the desk with me. I had only an instant to find something. The only things I could see in the shadows of the desk were a pistol butt and two of my clown bombs. I grabbed the pistol and tried to get one of the bombs out, but the wires connecting the switches to the bombs were hopelessly entangled. I pulled them both out, at the same time realizing that I had grabbed the blank pistol instead of the real one.

As J.D. went down, I threw the bombs toward Frankie, lying there on the floor, hoping one would get close enough to blind him for a second while I went for J.D.'s gun. But only one got close. The other fell halfway between. As Frankie aimed at J.D., I stood up and yelled, trying to press both of the bomb switches since I didn't know which one went to the one lying on the floor beside Frankie's head. One of the switches slipped out of my hand and landed on the desk. I pressed the remaining one.

The bomb halfway between me and Frankie went off. It didn't have any power, since it was designed to make noise and a lot of smoke. But it did get Frankie's attention. He fired at me and missed, but I heard a sharp intake of breath from Andy. I turned to look at the old man. His head slumped on his chest and I saw a spot of red appear on his white shirt, high up on his chest.

36

I heard Frankie's laugh about the time I felt the hot muzzle burn a round "O" brand into the back of my neck. I tensed, waiting for the blast.

Frankie's whole body shook as he laughed. He was delirious, or nearly so.

"Oh, this is great! Wonderful!" He laughed some more. "I was trying to figure a way to get rid of the old man so I could take over, but this is better than anything I ever dreamed up."

Out of the corner of my eye, I could see something black moving up and down behind my shoulder. Frankie straightened out his left hand and I could see that it was the electrician's tape-wrapped bomb that had fallen by his head. He was throwing it up in the air and catching it.

"So, were you going to kill me with this? A clown bomb?"

This time, he threw his head back and laughed, shaking his head. When he stopped, he ordered me to put the revolver on the desk. I did.

With my head turned slightly to the left, I could see him gloating over his victory. *God,* I thought, *if only I could reach the switch there on the desk.* The bomb wasn't that powerful, but each time he threw it up, it got within inches of his face. At that distance, it would at least blind him. But the switch was out of reach, and the muzzle of his gun was burning into the skin of my neck. It seemed like the only chance I had, but I knew Frankie was just waiting for me to move. I'd be dead before my hand ever reached the switch.

"Oh, this is fantastic. Now you'll be blamed for Dad's death, I'll be regarded as a hero for killing you, and that, along with being his son, will make me the natural choice to fill his shoes. I was going to use the disk as proof that the old man was getting soft, but I don't need it anymore, thanks to you. Things couldn't be better."

He stopped pitching the bomb up in the air and leaned closer to me. His breath was as hot in my ear as his gun muzzle was on my neck as he hissed at me.

"You're going to die, asshole. Maybe I'll have this little piece framed as a memento of the greatest moment in my life. Now turn around."

I did. He raised the bomb to his face to look at it as he moved back away from me, keeping his arm extended as he backed up and pointed the gun at my left eye. *To keep the powder and the brains from getting on him,* I thought. The gun muzzle's position would cause the bullet and brains to exit somewhere around the left rear quadrant of my skull, I calculated.

From the right bottom corner of my eye, I saw something white move. Then the explosion came.

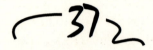

It was one of those moments when a second seems like minutes. The first thing I realized when the explosion came was that I was still thinking. The second was that it came from Frankie's left, not his right. The third was that my right ear felt like it had been blown off, and all I could hear was ringing on the right side. Funny, I thought, that I should feel the left side of my head being blown off but not feel the bullet enter. Fourth, I realized again that I was still thinking. And with that thought, I moved.

With my movement came the realization that I hadn't been shot. It had been the bomb going off. It seemed to take seconds for my hand to wrap around the grip of the pistol on the edge of the desk. It was only then that I saw the white toilet paper sticking out of the front of the cylinder and it registered in my brain that this was the blank pistol, not the Colt. No matter. There was no time for anything else. Another two or three seconds seemed to slip away as I raised it and turned. But I'd been a bullfighter and clown for too long to worry about the time it was taking.

Whenever I'd had to go in to save a hung-up bull rider,

time had slowed down this same way to allow my brain to better direct my body, which was still running at above-normal speed.

As I raised the gun, the time switch in my brain clicked again and everything returned to normal speed. Frankie, the whole left side of his face blackened and smoking, squinted through a red, watering right eye, bringing the big automatic to bear on my face even as I pointed my blank pistol at him. I had hoped that he'd be close enough I could stick the gun to his temple and fire it. Stuck to his head like that, there would be nowhere for the force of the discharge to go except into his skull. If it didn't kill him, it would at least stun him long enough for me to get away or disable him further. But he had taken a step back when the explosion occurred, and my only hope now was to blind his good eye with the powder and hopefully make him miss.

I fired. The black powder caused so much smoke that I couldn't see anything beyond my outstretched hand. I remembered reading somewhere that Civil War soldiers had had that same problem, being blinded by the smoke after firing their muzzleloaders. At the same time, I heard the report of a .45 somewhere on the other side of the smoke. Again I tensed for the impact that never came.

As the smoke slowly dissipated, Frankie's face came into view. There was a gaping hole where his left eye had been, and bits of something mucous-like showed behind the white bone and red blood. The right eye looked unbelieving at me for a fraction of a second before it closed for the third and final time that night.

Frankie fell forward, and I sidestepped to let him topple to the floor. More smoke cleared, and out of a mistlike background stepped an angel. And the angel's name was Alisa.

She dropped her smoking gun to the floor and rushed to me. I held her tighter than I'd ever held anything in my

George Wilhite 155

life. Together we turned toward the desk and were greeted by the pale but smiling face of Andy, his left hand still lying on the bomb switch, a band of white dress shirt extending from the cuff of his jacket. That cuff had been the white flash I'd seen out of the corner of my eye.

Behind him, J.D. was getting to his feet, his hand to his left shoulder.

Feebly, Andy motioned us to him. "I'm okay. I've been shot before. This one is too high up to be dangerous. I'll phone for help. You leave here. Now."

Alisa started to protest. The old man forced the tone of authority into his voice.

"NOW! I'll take care of this. Everyone here is loyal to me except the three lying on the floor. I've had my suspicions about Frankie for some time, but I didn't want to admit it. There's no doubt now. I heard everything he said after I was shot." He seemed to be gaining strength, overcoming the initial shock of the gunshot. "As for the disk, don't worry about it. The story won't need to come out. We'll pull out of the sport. It had gotten out of hand anyway. It used to be just a way for down-and-out cowboys at some of the East Coast rodeos to get back home. That's the only reason I ever started it."

He looked down at his dead son and sighed.

"He never got it. There's more to being a cowboy than riding and roping and being wild."

He looked up at me, and glanced at his daughter in my arms.

"As for Alisa, she never knew what I did for a living until Frankie came along. Both she and I heard about Jake's death after it happened. Don't let that bother you."

Alisa moved to her father and hugged him, then planted a lingering kiss on his forehead. She let her head slip down onto his shoulder, mindful of the wound.

"But I killed Frankie, Daddy. Can you forgive me for that?"

I spoke up before he could respond. "You didn't kill him, Alisa. I did. You missed. It was my bullet that killed your brother."

She looked at me, then back at her father. He nodded and smiled. She wiped a tear away and stood up, reaching out for my hand.

As we turned away, I looked at Andy. Our eyes met. He glanced down at my pistol lying on his desk. It was turned so that he could see the white toilet paper sticking out of the chambers in the cylinder; he knew there were no bullets in the gun, only powder. Looking back up at me, a wry smile played across his pale lips. Then his hand came up and motioned us to go.

38

J.D., Alisa, and I slipped out of the mansion unnoticed and made it to the truck. J.D. threw our bags into the back and slipped in the passenger's door, leaving me and Alisa alone for a moment. For just a second, we clung to each other. Even through her evening gown, I could feel her softness. Her long and slender fingers came up to my face, and she pulled my chin to hers, kissing me hard and full of lust. I should have picked her up and carried her off to live happily ever after.

But the fingers, the kiss—they were all wrong. I'd felt strongly for this woman once, still did. But something was missing. This love, strong as it was, wasn't the right one. We were from two completely different worlds.

"Alisa, what do you do for a living?"

Her head pulled back a little and tilted to one side, questioning.

"I'm a corporate lawyer in Boston. I was accepted into law school right after you left."

"Big practice?"

"Yes."

"Pretty good income?"

She pulled back a bit further, dropped her chin, and raised a perfectly made-up eyebrow. "Yes."

"Be kind of hard to leave there, wouldn't it?"

"What are you getting at, Ira?"

I stroked my hand along her perfect jawline, the soft white skin so pleasant to touch. I shook my head.

"I loved you once . . . maybe I still do. But I have no desire to live in Boston. There are no rodeos. And would you move to Hillsboro, or Waco, or Dallas, and give up your practice?"

I could see the doubt in her eyes. "I think I could."

Again I shook my head. "No, Alisa. We both fell in love with someone from another world, someone so different from most of the people we knew that we were intrigued by them, by the romance of it all. I was a Wild West cowboy, you were the big-city sophisticate. We were all caught up in the exoticness of it all, like a fairytale. But that's not what makes marriages last, and we both know it."

She looked down at the ground, and I heard a sniffle. But her head came up quickly, and there were no tears in her eyes.

"You know, I think you're right. All the city men I've dated have been pretty bland. After tonight, they'll be even more so. But it would be hard on us."

She held my face for a moment.

"If you ever need a good lawyer—even if you're old, fat, and baldheaded with a wife and six kids—you call me, okay?"

I nodded, smiling. "And if you ever need an old, broken-down rodeo clown or a pretty good English teacher, you call."

We pulled each other close and our lips met. Just as quickly, we moved apart, until only the tips of our outstretched fingers were touching. Then she turned and ran gracefully toward the mansion. I watched her until she

George Wilhite 159

was inside. I felt a hard lump in my chest that made me think I hadn't made the right choice. But second by second, a light, warm feeling replaced it. I knew I had done the right thing. I opened the driver's side door and climbed into the pickup. J.D. was sitting with his head against the side window, his hat pulled over his face, seemingly oblivious to everything that had just happened.

I switched on the engine and sat looking out across the Llano River.

J.D. shuffled a little and lifted the brim of his hat with one finger, just enough to look out at me with his left eye.

"Well, boss, where we going from here?"

I put the truck in gear and started forward, heading east. "Home. I got to see a vet about a heart problem."

39

We stopped at the low-water crossing on the Llano River long enough to change out of our clowning togs, wash J.D.'s wound with bottled water, glob a bunch of antibiotic cream on it, and wrap it with a gauze pad and an Ace bandage. Fortunately, the bullet had merely dug a furrow in his muscle. If it had been a puncture wound, even if it had gone all the way through, we'd have had to find a doctor to be sure it was treated right.

J.D. fell into a deep sleep as soon as we got back on the road. I knew that Chelsey was probably just starting back from East Texas and probably had a little farther to go than we did, but I figured we'd head for her place, not mine. Then, when she came in, she could make sure J.D.'s wound was patched okay.

Looking out the side window, I caught the slight smile on my face in the reflection as I thought about how I'd rather have her, a horse doctor, working on me than most of the human doctors I knew. Griz excepted, of course.

I kept catching myself speeding on the farm-to-market roads between Llano and the interstate, anxious to get back even though I knew Chelsey wouldn't be there yet. I cut through the Hill Country to Georgetown, just above Austin, and hit Interstate 35, smooth and wide in the moonlight. Falling in behind a convoy of truckers, I managed to keep a constant 85 mph most of the way.

I had a lot of time to think in the two-hour drive back to West. I'd killed a man tonight. Actually, I pulled the trigger on a gun loaded with blanks, but only because I'd picked up the wrong gun. I'd been ready to kill him from the moment he admitted he'd pulled the trigger on Jake. I knew he would kill me without a moment's thought, the hatred in him seething to the surface like an active volcano. But it still didn't sit right. I hadn't hesitated. I hadn't blinked an eye. In a way, it was a lot like fighting bulls. You don't think about the danger, the moral implications, or whether the guy you're saving is sleeping with your wife. You just jump in and do what is necessary. In bullfighting, the job is to save a cowboy's life; tonight the job had been to take one's life. And I hadn't flinched. It was, as I'd heard in movies, a "righteous kill," and I wasn't sorry that Frankie wouldn't hurt anyone anymore. But I was sorry that there hadn't been some other way to solve the problem.

Somewhere between Temple and Waco, I came to the realization that, despite my misgivings about the matter, I was glad that he was taken care of.

J.D. was asleep, snoring slightly. I wondered what the deal would be with the magazine, now that Jake was gone. The last month's issue had just gone out about a week before Jake's death. Another would need to be in production in the next week or two. By rights, J.D. should get the magazine, but I wasn't sure what precautions Jake had taken—will, insurance, that kind of thing. I hoped he had left something written somewhere so that J.D. didn't have a court battle on his hands.

The magazine had made Jake an okay living, but he

hadn't been getting rich. He'd concentrated only on Texas rodeos, and so he wasn't ever able to attract any national advertising. We'd talked before about his going national, but he said the 800-plus rodeos held in Texas were more than enough to keep him busy. If there wasn't a nest egg somewhere, a court fight could be the death knell for the publication. I decided right then and there that I would offer J.D. whatever help I could in getting the magazine back on its feet, even canceling clowning jobs if I had to.

We pulled into a Diamond Shamrock on the north side of Waco about 3:00 A.M., and I grabbed us a couple of Irish cream flavored coffees. We only had about fifteen miles left to go to get to Chelsey's place on the south side of West, near the auction barn. J.D. was still asleep, so I set his coffee in the cup holder and headed north on the last leg of the trip home.

I was glad to finally pull into the yard in front of Chelsey's office. A quick check of the empty yard showed no red Dodge Dually with its almost ever-present horse trailer.

To the right of the parking area was a huge, U-shaped building that housed the stables area with its enclosed stalls. The open end of the U faced the parking lot and, directly across from it, the picture window at the front of Chelsey's house. She could look out that window and see the stables from the dining area behind the window and the living area that opened onto the dining room. She had a sort of sixth sense about animals in trouble. I'd quit counting the near-intimate evenings that had been interrupted by the quick swing of her head toward that window and the hushed "Shhh!" that preceded a night spent at the stables with a colicky horse or a heifer having trouble calving.

The dash clock showed 3:20 A.M. Chelsey would probably arrive in about an hour, maybe less. She'd said she was entered in the show and would be heading out as soon as she was through, leaving instructions on where to mail the check if she was in the money. One advantage of having a thriving vet business during the week was that, unlike many of the competitors on the road, she didn't have to wait around for the money after a show just to get on to the next rodeo or to get home. That was the last thought I had before I drifted off into a well-deserved sleep behind the wheel, making a short mental note that J.D. was still asleep on his side of the cab.

Something woke me up and, for a minute, I wasn't sure what it was. The dash clock showed 3:50 A.M. I blinked my eyes a couple of times, looked around the empty cab, then remembered that I hadn't checked my answering machine at home. I pulled the cell phone out of the console and punched in my home phone number. Four rings later, the machine answered, I tapped in the code and listened to the two messages.

One was from some lawyer in Dallas. The name rang a bell, but I couldn't quite place it. I jotted down the number and went on to the second message. As it started, I noticed the headlights in the side mirror. They pulled up directly behind me, shining right into my eyes. Still half asleep, I wondered why Chelsey had slammed the door and was running toward the cab of my truck. As I opened the door, I heard the second message. It was Alisa, her voice breathless with excitement and worry.

"Ira, you're in danger!" she said. "One of Frankie's friends got away. He walked in as I got back to Dad, saw Frankie's body, and ran out before we could stop him. I think he's coming after you. If you get this message, don't go home. Call us and we'll get some folks up there to take care of the situation. But be careful. And call us."

I was so taken aback by the message that I just sat there with my hand on the half-opened door. My brain was still sleep-soggy, but two things fought their way to my consciousness now that I'd heard the message. First, I hadn't heard that familiar throbbing sound of Chelsey's diesel truck as she pulled into the gate. Second, the shadow coming toward my truck didn't look especially feminine. I was trying to get the message to close the door from my brain to my arm when the door was jerked out of my hand and a big, hairy paw grabbed my collar and pulled me out of the cab.

The hooking and the fighting and the lack of sleep had taken their toll. I swung a weak right at the thug who had collared me, but he swept it aside with his left hand, laughed, and smacked me with a staggering jab that felt like it slammed my right eye into the back of my skull. Then everything went black.

Sometime later I came to and tried to raise my hand to my head, where red and yellow fireworks sent pain deep into my brain. But my hand wouldn't move. I was dimly aware of light through barely opened eyes, so I tried to blink and open them. The left one worked fine, but the right one barely parted. As the fireworks subsided, I could feel a throbbing pain in my right eye and the puffy pressure that comes from a swelling eyelid. With my good eye, I looked around the room.

I was in one of Chelsey's examination/operating rooms, standing against a metal rack in the middle of the concrete floor, the one used to contain horses for examinations, shots, or minor operations. It was made of three-inch steel pipe. With my left eye, I could see that my arms were tied to the rack with the soft cotton ropes Chelsey used to tie horses when necessary.

All the lights were on, and I could barely see someone standing in front of the row of medical equipment on the wall to my right. When he turned around, I recognized him, despite my bad vision. It was Steve Holmes, the *Texas Rodeo* field editor. The one J.D. said was with the Mafia. He was obviously the friend of Frankie's who had gotten away from the mansion in Llano.

Even more recognizable than Steve was the tool he was holding when he turned to me. Long-handled, it looked like a bolt-cutter, and that's pretty much what it was, but a specialized version called a burdizzo. Whereas bolt-cutters are sharp, burdizzos are blunted. They weren't made for cutting cleanly through metal but for mashing flesh and blood vessels. Their special, workaday purpose was to castrate bull calves at roundup. From the look Holmes had on his face, I was sure it wasn't bull calves he was meaning to work on.

He came toward me with the long-handled tool, a sneer—twisted and wicked—on his lips and his eyes squinted with hate.

"You sumbitch," he said, his speech slurred and slow. "You screwed up everthin' for me, you know."

The man was drunk. Not incapacitated, but well under the influence of alcohol and who knows what else. He'd probably been at the party enjoying himself before Frankie's death changed his whole world.

Steve had been a good steer dogger once, and the nearly 300 pounds he carried now had once been solid muscle. But he'd had a reputation for gambling and boozing. It hadn't taken long before he'd dropped out of the standings and had gone to work for Jake at the magazine. Jake had tolerated him because the big man knew the timed events better than almost anyone, and he still had a lot of friends. It didn't take a big stretch to imagine Frankie being one of them, especially if he'd pulled the same deal on Holmes that he'd pulled on J.D.

George Wilhite 167

There was blood on the man's white shirt front that I figured must have come from my nose and eye when he hit me. One shirttail was out of his pants and a big green streak of snot ran down on one sleeve where he'd wiped his nose. He held the burdizzo up and clicked it like hedge shears as he got closer.

"I didn't know Frankie was going to shoot the old geezer when we come to the office that day," he said. "It wasn't my fault. But Frankie was good to me."

I spat on the floor between us and tried to give him as good a go-to-hell look as I could with my one good eye.

"Frankie played you like one of them *charros* plays a forefooted horse in a *charreada.* Jake gave you a job when nobody else would."

He laughed a bitter, mean laugh. "Hell, I was already working for Frankie. He knew the old fart had the info for a story, so he said I should just play along and make myself useful. Find out where the old man had the stuff. As soon as I knew, I called Frankie."

He clicked the castrating tool again. I looked him square in the eye.

"Holmes, you better do more than use them on my nuts. You better kill me. Because if you leave me alive, I won't rest until you've been brought to justice. Not legal justice . . . cowboy justice."

He was only about ten feet away when I heard the horn honk. Holmes' head shot up, and he ran to cover my mouth with his thick hand. After the last of the horn's noise died away, all I could hear was the labored breathing of the former steer wrestler, his face and fetid breath only inches from my nose and ear. Then, faintly, I heard the throb of a diesel engine pulling into the driveway. And then another round of honking.

Jesus Christ, I thought, *it's Chelsey!* Despite the pain it caused, I tried to jerk my mouth from behind Holmes' hand, but he ground his thumb into my already closed eye, and the red and yellow fireworks came back, accompanied by a nauseous feeling that quickly turned into a raging, gagging wad of acid in my mouth. And I blacked out for the second time.

41

I was conscious again in what must have been a few seconds. Holmes was tying his bandanna across my mouth, gagging me to keep me quiet. The horn honked again, and the diesel engine murmured to a stop. For just a second, there was nothing. Just as quickly as silence had come, it was gone. Chelsey's voice came through the two partially opened barn doors comprising the wall of her examining room that opened to the parking area.

"Ira! I'm home. What are you doing in the examining room? Someone got a sick animal in there?"

I could tell from her voice that she was still out near my truck. She couldn't have gotten around it to pull up to the stables. I had to find some way to warn her. I struggled against the ropes that held me to the rack, but they were tight and didn't budge. If only I could get to the clip knife I kept in my right rear Wranglers pocket. But I couldn't.

Holmes reached under the shirttail that was hanging out of his pants and brought out a big, black, automatic pistol. He glanced at me, smirked, then stepped out into the parking area. The son of a bitch was going to kill Chelsey, the woman I loved, and there was not a damned thing I could do to stop it. Hot tears stung my swollen eye. Nothing I could do. If only J.D. were here . . .

That thought jerked my head up and stopped the tears. Where the hell was J.D.? He'd been asleep in the passenger's seat when I fell asleep earlier. But he'd been gone when I woke up at 3:50. I glanced around the room. A big round clock with a huge second hand hung high on the opposite wall. It was 4:05—fifteen minutes since Holmes had smacked me in the face and hauled me in here. Somewhere between fifteen and forty-five minutes since J.D. was asleep in my truck. Where the hell was he?

At that exact moment, something touched my hands behind my back. I snapped my neck around. There, in all his glory, stood John Davis, former saddle bronc riding champion, a silly smile on his face. The smile broadened as he held up a pocketknife for me to see. Then, with a wink, he bent over to start cutting my bonds.

I felt one of the ropes part, and I jerked my hand free to grab my gag as J.D. stooped to cut the ropes holding my feet to the bottom of the rack. I had one hand on the gag when I heard it. The crack of a solitary gunshot in the still night air. My heart sank, but my hand pulled the gag out of my mouth just as the last rope on my legs fell away.

"Damnit . . . Chelsey!" I hollered as I started at a run for the door.

I'd only taken one step when a figure burst through the opening. In a pair of blue Lawman jeans and a white satin blouse with fringe down both sleeves, Chelsey never slowed between the door and me. She slammed into me, forcing me back against the rack, but I wasn't complaining. She was talking and I was mumbling; kisses and tears were going everywhere. With both of my arms around her and holding tight, I slumped to the floor, taking her with me. We sat there and just held each other for quite a while. About the time I realized that my heart had started beating again, I saw Tommy Adwell, Jake's old friend who had offered help at the funeral, step through the doorway. His lever-action .45-70 rested in the crook of his arm.

Tommy grabbed the door and shoved it open all the way. The light spilled out into the parking area to reveal Steve Holmes lying on his back in the white gravel lot, holding his leg and moaning to beat hell. The hole didn't look the size of a softball, but I wasn't about to mention it to Tommy. He looked around the examining room.

"Damn," he said, looking back at the three of us while shoving the dogger's automatic into his belt, "you ain't got no salt here?"

42

I was sitting on the sofa in my living room, my head lying on Chelsey's shoulder as she spoon-fed me some fresh stew she'd just made. J.D. was in the kitchen, getting reaquainted with his wife and kids by phone. Bill Lee sat across the coffee table on the big, brown overstuffed leather club chair that didn't go with a damned thing in my living room. He was hunched forward, writing down the last of our comments in the little notebook he kept in his chest pocket.

"So," he said, "you're telling me that, while you were asleep, J.D. had to pee and got out of the truck?"

Chelsey fed me another spoonful of stew, then pointed the spoon at Bill before dropping it into the now-empty stew bowl.

"That's right, Chief Lee. He was around the side of the stables when Holmes pulled Ira from the truck. J.D. had taken a couple of pretty good hookings at the Llano rodeo and knew he was in no shape to take a heavyweight on."

She conveniently left out the part about J.D.'s gunshot

wound. J.D. had hung up the phone in the kitchen and stood leaning against the doorway. He chimed in.

"About then, I headed for the auction barn and the café there."

"The Czech-American Restaurant?" Bill asked, writing it all down.

"Yes, sir," J.D. said. "It's not 300 yards from the vet clinic, and I knew they were open twenty-four hours and that I might even be able to find someone to help me there. I was planning on calling you, Bill, and then getting back to help Ira. But Mr. Adwell had gathered cattle the evening before, kept 'em in a pen, watered 'em, and then loaded 'em early in the morning so they wouldn't dry out and lose weight during the heat of the day. Good thing for us that he was dropping them off there so early. When I got to the auction barn, I saw his truck and trailer and Chelsey's side by side. Chelsey had stopped to talk to him before pulling on down the road to her place."

Chelsey set the empty bowl on the end table, put both arms around my shoulders, and snuggled down even closer than she had been.

"We didn't have but a minute to come up with a plan, so I called 9-1-1 and told them there was a break-in at my clinic," she said, leaning her head against the good side of my head and avoiding the ice pack I had on my right eye. "We didn't know if we'd have time to wait for a cop or not, Bill. We figured I'd pull up, honk and holler while J.D. snuck around the other side of the clinic and used my key to let himself in another door, and get Ira out of there. Mr. Adwell pulled out that lever gun and was off to one side of me to protect me when Holmes came out. The bastard came out and pointed the gun at me. Mr. Adwell shot him. He was protecting my life."

Bill closed his notebook and stuffed it back into his pocket.

"No problem there," he said. "Steve Holmes has been

in trouble ever since he started gambling ten years ago. Up to then, he'd been a pretty good cowboy, but after that he just kept slidin' farther and farther. I imagine he'll get a pretty tough sentence as an accessory to murder and for attempted murder. From y'all's accounts, it seems like a case of self-defense on y'all's part."

He stood, gathered his hat from the antler hat rack by the door, and left with a curt goodbye.

J.D. sat down in the club chair opposite us and held up an envelope.

"Found this on the kitchen table," he said, eyeing it critically. "Some lawyer from Dallas. You might ought to open it." He flipped it to me and I caught it.

"I don't know any lawyers in Dallas," I said, reaching into my back pocket to pull out my clip knife. As I slit the top of the envelope, four or five sheets of expensive paper fell out on my lap. I picked them up and unfolded them. The words at the top caught my eye.

"Last Will and Testament . . ."

It was Jake's will. I read a little further, then dropped the paper and shook my head at J.D.

"No, J.D., I can't do this. It ain't right."

J.D. smiled and held a hand up. "It's right, Ira. It's what Jake wanted to do."

"But the magazine is yours, not mine. I have no right to it. You do."

"Look, I have no idea how to run the damned thing. He left me the press, which I don't know how to run either. But I figure that with you owning the magazine and me owning the press, we could form some sort of partnership. The lawyer agreed. What do you say?"

When I looked at Chelsey, she nodded. I ducked my head and took a deep breath, then let out a long sigh.

"Well, hell, I guess so."

J.D. and I stood up and shook on it. Then I looked over

his shoulder at the *Texas Rodeo* calendar I'd gotten from Jake in December, hanging on the opposite wall.

"Damn," I said, "is it really the twenty-first?"

J.D. turned around and looked at the calendar, too. "Yep. Month's almost over."

I dropped my ice pack on the coffee table and tried to step around Chelsey. "We got a magazine to put out and only about seven days to do it in. We need to get to work. Pronto."

But the lady horse doctor grabbed me by the back of my belt and jerked me down on the couch beside her. Then she swung one leg over me and straddled me on the couch. With expert care, she cupped my face in both her hands and made me look her right in the eye.

"He won't be working today, J.D.! Why don't you take the keys to my place and get a little rest?" she called over her shoulder, never taking her eyes off me. He laughed, grabbed the keys, and headed for the door.

"What about him?" he asked, the door already open.

"Yeah," I said, "what about me?"

She squeezed me just a little harder with those thighs made strong by countless hours in the saddle and kept my face close to hers in those cupped, not-so-soft hands. I breathed in the aroma of her perfume, felt the soft and gentle touch of her fingers, remembered the kiss that woke me up in the morning—and finally, I knew. These were the right ones. I looked into her face and saw it all there.

"He'll meet you at the magazine tomorrow," she said. "But right now, I've got to tend to my patient."

J.D. was smiling as he closed the door, and somewhere underneath the jean-and-T-shirt-clad body of Dr. Leskowitz, so was I.

About
the
Author

George Wilhite learned the ropes of rodeoing as a bareback rider (thirteen years), bull rider (eight years), rodeo clown and bullfighter (ten years), and rodeo photographer (twenty years). He was named to the board of the Texas Rodeo Cowboy Hall of Fame in 2003.

Wilhite is a former editor of *Rodeo News,* the International Professional Rodeo Association's magazine (now *Pro Rodeo World*), and was the *Rodeo News* photographer at the International Finals Rodeo in 1980 and 1981 (IFR10 and IFR11) as well as at the Madison Square Garden Rodeo in 1981. He also has served as the official photographer of the Texas Police Officers Rodeo Association Finals Rodeo and was selected as the official photographer for the World Finals Rodeo in the mid-1990s. His photos have been featured on the cover of *Rodeo News, Rodeo Times, Rodeo Illustrated,* and *Texas Rodeo,* and in *Western Horseman* magazine. Some of his photos can be seen on his Texas Rodeo website (www.texasrodeo.go.to).

The author holds bachelor's and master's degrees in English from the University of Texas at San Antonio. He is currently a writing instructor at Texas State Technical College in Waco and is an active member of the Mystery Western Writers of America. The veteran journalist has been a reporter, photographer, editor, and publisher.

Two of his rodeo short stories were published in *American Western* magazine (www.readthewest.com): "Jonas," which was nominated for a 2002 Spur Award, and "Red Malone." Another rodeo short story, "Midget," was also nominated for a Spur. His short story "Coronas 'n Crawfish" will appear in the MWA anthology *Fedora III* in 2004. The second in the Texas Rodeo Mystery Series, *Dead in the Heart O' Texas,* is in the works, as is a historical rodeo murder mystery.